Hidden Darkness

The Chronicles of Kerrigan, Volume 7

W.J. May

Published by Wanita May, 2016.

D1519785

The Chronicles of Kerrigan

Hidden Darkness

Book VII

By

Copyright 2016 by W.J. May

Also by W.J. May

Hidden Darkness

The Chronicles of Kerrigan Prequel
Christmas Before the Magic

The Hidden Secrets Saga
Seventh Mark (part 1 & 2)

The Senseless Series
Radium Halos
Radium Halos - Part 2
Nonsense

The X Files
Replica X

Standalone
Shadow of Doubt (Part 1 & 2)
Five Shades of Fantasy
Glow - A Young Adult Fantasy Sampler
Shadow of Doubt - Part 2
Four and a Half Shades of Fantasy
Full Moon
Dream Fighter
What Creeps in the Night
Forest of the Forbidden
HuNted
Arcane Forest: A Fantasy Anthology
Ancient Blood of the Vampire and Werewolf

The Chronicles of Kerrigan

Book I - *Rae of Hope* is FREE!
   Book Trailer:
   http://www.youtube.com/watch?v=gILAwXxx8MU
   Book II - *Dark Nebula*
   Book Trailer:
   http://www.youtube.com/watch?v=Ca24STi_bFM
   Book III - *House of Cards*
   Book IV - *Royal Tea*
   Book V - *Under Fire*
   Book VI - *End in Sight*
   Book VII – *Hidden Darkness*
   Book VIII – *Twisted Together*
   COMING FEBRUARY 2016
   PREQUEL – Christmas Before the Magic

Coming Christmas 2015!!

A Novella of the Chronicles of Kerrigan.
A prequel on how Simon Kerrigan met Beth!!
AVAILABLE:

Find W.J. May

Website:
http://www.wanitamay.yolasite.com
Facebook:
https://www.facebook.com/pages/Author-WJ-May-FAN-
PAGE/141170442608149
Newsletter:
SIGN UP FOR W.J. May's Newsletter to find out about new
releases, updates, cover reveals and even freebies!
http://eepurl.com/97aYf

Description:

Hidden Darkness is the 7th Book of W.J. May's bestselling series, The Chronicles of Kerrigan.

A race against time, a sprint across the world.

The enemy has a new face now, Jonathon Cromfield. Except he's not really new, is he?

Cromfield has a plan, one that includes Rae whether she likes it or not.

Rae is terrified by the idea that she can't die. Everyone she'll ever know will move on without her and leave her all alone. Except Cromfield. She'd rather die than be with him.

The team of Rae, Devon, Julian and Molly must race around the world to find the hybrids before Cromfield does, they have to figure out what his serum really is for, and take it back to the Privy Council all before Cromfield can stop them.

Immortal or not, Rae doesn't have a second to waste.

Hidden Darkness is the 7th book in the Chronicles of Kerrigan series.

Book 1, Rae of Hope is currently FREE.

Follow Rae Kerrigan as she learns about the tattoo on her back that gives her supernatural powers, as she learns of her father's evil intentions and as she tries to figure out how coming of age, falling love and high-packed action fighting isn't as easy as the comic books make it look.

Series Order:

Rae of Hope

Dark Nebula

House of Cards

Royal Tea

Under Fire
End in Sight
Hidden Darkness
Twisted Together
Prequel: Christmas Before the Magic

W.J. May

TABLE OF CONTENTS

'The only thing wrong with immortality is that it tends to go on forever.'
Herb Caen

Chapter 1

I couldn't have said it better myself. Eternity's never going to end.

"Rae! Please calm down!"

Devon streaked out of the room after her; up out of the tomb, through the maze of catacombs, into the cemetery beyond. Only he had a chance of catching her, with his unique gift of speed. Except even he had a hard time keeping pace with her—eyes straining in the darkness to latch onto the occasional glint of her dark hair as she flew out ahead. No one else would have been a problem, but Rae had gifts of her own. And, apparently, more than any of them had bargained for.

"Sweetheart, slow down!" he yelled as he ran. "Come back! We'll figure this out!"

He didn't know how it was true. What could they possibly do? The love of his life was going to live forever. While he and everyone else they knew would slowly age and die.

It was a curse—he'd decided it the moment he heard the word.

And, by the looks of things, it appeared that Rae had, too.

"Kerrigan—*please*!"

He slipped back into the name he'd called her during their first year. The one where he was trying to keep his distance and play the part of the neutral mentor. Last names had helped then. So had the fact that two people like them—people with abilities—were absolutely forbidden from any kind of romantic entanglement.

That hadn't stopped them, though; nor had the successive years of fighting off people bent on killing her. Neither had the evil madman come back from the dead to claim her, nor had his own father turning him out in the cold.

But now this?

A sudden waft of wet city streets hit him in the face, and he pulled in a gasping breath, searching around as he tried to locate Rae. Most times, his heightened senses were his greatest asset, pointing him true North, keeping him alive again and again. But sometimes, times such as these, it was almost overwhelming. He could hear a cab driver bargaining with a woman four blocks over. He could smell the faint reek of sewage running beneath them through the city pipes. He could see every single one of the midnight rain drops as they splashed onto the drenched pavement.

But the location of the one person he wanted to find? That was a mystery.

A quiet sob cued him in. He whirled around at the speed of light, and doubled back the way he'd come. A tiny figure squatted beneath a lone streetlight, staring out at the passing cars. She was wearing a black jacket and her arms were wrapped tight around her, as if she could ward off the coming storm literally by holding herself together amidst the waves.

He was beside her in a moment. "Rae..." He stared entreatingly in her eyes. Eyes that always had time for him. He could make those eyes laugh, or cry, or melt into little pools of happiness. After all this time, he knew them as well as his own.

But right now...he doubted if they could even see him.

They were fixed on the blur of headlights streaking past on the darkened street, watching each one as it passed on into the night. Her eyes weren't just distracted; they were different, too. Harder. As if, despite the sudden irony of this statement, she had abruptly aged past her years.

For a moment, he simply stared, re-memorizing her familiar face; watching as the steady fall of rain trickled down her fair skin.

How could it be that she would never die? How could they fight something like this? Something that didn't have a face or an agenda? Something that simply had...her?

"Rae! Devon!"

Julian and Molly were out of the cemetery now, tearing towards them down the street. Luke had started automatically running with them, but Molly said something into his ear, and, the next second, he vanished around the corner. Devon glanced their way, eyes silently urging them to be careful. Rae was not herself right now. In fact, he wasn't sure quite who she was. But the look on Julian's face in particular frightened him, and he turned quickly back around—only to see Rae suddenly standing several yards away.

"Rae?" he mirrored his friends' call tentatively, trying to gauge where she was.

Julian and Molly's shouts had snapped her out of her trance, and she was staring at the cars with a very different expression now. One that Devon didn't quite know how to place. There was a moment where time seemed to suspend—where even the raindrops paused in their fall—and then she was a blur of speed.

Her eyes filled with sudden hysteria as she went tearing out into the road. She was using Devon's own tatù, so he didn't even realize what was happening until it was almost too late.

He saw the truck coming in slow motion, Rae standing before it with her arms open wide.

"NO!"

Tatù or no tatù, he had never moved so fast in his life. Not even the rain could catch him as he went barreling out into the road, throwing his body in between her and the truck, tackling her to safety.

Molly's scream echoed in the night as they landed hard on the wet pavement on the other side of the street. Devon's hand shot out to catch Rae's head, but she was already on her feet, watching the truck race away into the night with a grim expression settling on her face.

"What the hell do you think you're doing?!" Devon grabbed her by the shoulders, trying to literally shake her out of it. "Are you crazy?! You could have been killed!"

At these last words, she finally turned to him, seeing him for the first time. Her eyes met his, but he didn't find the relief he was hoping for. Instead, he felt more distant than ever. It was like there was a strange darkness inside of her, pulling her someplace he couldn't follow.

"But it wouldn't have, would it?"

She wasn't talking to him. She was talking to Julian. He and Molly had finally caught up with them, dodging their way across the street, and were staring at her in a kind of dulled horror.

Julian didn't answer her question. Instead, he looked guiltily away, not wanting to say it.

She nodded knowingly, but then suddenly crossed the space in between them and turned his face towards her sharply. His eyes glassed over against his will as she started scrolling through a list in her head. One scenario after another. Each as gruesome as the next.

Devon stood frozen in place, shivering without realizing it in the rain, while Molly whimpered quietly beside him. For a moment, neither of them knew what to do.

Then Julian groaned softly, pulling his face away. "Don't! Don't make me see this." He covered his eyes with his hands and she finally let up, taking a small step back.

Rae's breathing was quick, shallow, like she'd just run a marathon. She kept her eyes locked on Julian. When she finally spoke, her voice was quiet but firm. "Nothing works, does it?"

Julian's face tightened for a moment, bracing against a thousand horrible images of his friend's would-be death, but he shook his head. "Nothing works. You'd always survive."

Molly reached for her hand with tears in her eyes. "Rae, please, let's just go home and—"

But Rae was in her own little world, eyes fixed on something none of the rest of them could see. "I'm stuck here forever. Just me and Cromfield. Forever."

Those were the last words she said in London.

The other three piled her into the car and raced back to Guilder as fast as the rain would allow them. Molly sat up in front with Julian, while Devon perched hesitantly in the back, watching Rae with cautious, fearful eyes.

Rae, for one, seemed like she didn't have a care in the world. She just stared out the window of the car, tracing absentminded shapes in the steam on the glass as they flew out of the city.

It was shock, Devon decided. It was just shock, and it would wear off, and she would be fine. They would all be fine. They simply *had* to be.

But deep down...he didn't know how that could possibly be true.

Rae's new 'condition' notwithstanding, he'd seen the pictures just like everyone else. He'd seen the evidence of Cromfield's crimes. The mangled mothers' bodies. The bloodied infants, too powerful and too unstable to take more than a few shaky breaths in this world. He'd seen the bruised injection sites where Cromfield had tested his newfound serum on the caged hybrids. He'd seen the fatal results.

And now there was this list. Another round of mixed tatùs up for the slaughter. They had to save them. They had to get to them before Cromfield did. Devon knew this. He knew it with every fiber of his being. And yet...

He peered at Rae sitting in the moonlight beside him, tracing clovers on the window. The only thing he could bring himself to care about in the whole world was the girl sitting beside him. His heart tightened, and he realized the dark truth. He would sacrifice all the hybrids to save her. He would sacrifice everything he had.

Yet it wouldn't be enough.

It wasn't until the car pulled back into the Guilder parking lot that the four friends looked around at each other for the first time. The second day of graduation after-parties was still in full swing. It seemed impossible, they thought, as they watched their school friends drinking and laughing carelessly as they made their way across the sweeping lawns. It seemed impossible that they could be carrying on as if nothing had happened. As if their world hadn't been shaken to its very core.

"I can't go in there."

It was the first thing Rae had said in over an hour, and the other three jumped to attention as they turned around to look at her. Molly and Julian were frozen, no idea what to do next, but Devon tentatively took her hand, squeezing it gently in his own.

"Of course. That's just fine." He squeezed again. "Where do you want to go? What would make you feel better? To your new apartment back in London?" He stifled a shudder along with the rest of them. He didn't want to go anywhere near London and its secret lair of horrors right now. But, of course, if that's what Rae wanted—

"What're you talking about?" she asked sharply, turning to him with a frown. "Why would we go back to London—all our stuff is here."

Devon shared a quick look with the others. "Yeah...I just thought...what do you mean, *stuff*? Is there something you'd like?"

Rae glanced around the car in bewilderment, like she couldn't believe they were even having this discussion. "Well, I assumed we'd need to pack stuff for the trip. We're going to be gone for a long time."

Julian's eyes glassed over for a moment while Molly leaned forward with a concerned frown. "What trip? What're you talking about, Rae?"

"She wants to go find them," Julian said softly. Devon and Molly turned to him in shock, but his dark eyes were fixed on Rae with a look of utmost sympathy. "She's already decided."

"Of course I want to find them," Rae repeated in the same hard, incredulous voice. "They're going to *die*. We need to get to them before Cromfield does."

When no one said anything, Rae threw up her hands in exasperation. "What did you guys think we were going to do? Take this to the Privy Council? Carter already told us that they wouldn't believe the Cromfield story. They won't help us— they'd probably have us committed for telling such a crazy tale."

"But there's evidence now," Molly said softly. Her eyes tightened, as she both remembered and tried not to remember what they had seen in the lair. "We can take them back to the church—"

"There's no evidence of *Cromfield* being there," Rae reiterated. "There's just a list of hybrids, and, to be perfectly honest, with how the PC feels about people like me, I don't think giving them that list of names would help anybody on it. This is up to us."

Devon and Julian seemed to be having a silent communication on the other side of the car. Devon looked worried, while Julian looked resigned. When they finally turned back to the girls, Devon ran his hands through his hair with a sigh. "You really want to go do this? Now? I mean, you don't want to take a little time to—"

"All I have is time," Rae cut him off briskly. "This isn't about me. It's about them. We need to find them...*now*."

"How're we even going to know where to look?" Molly asked desperately. "There were over twenty people on that list. Cromfield could be headed to any one of them."

Rae turned deliberately to Julian. "Then good thing we know someone who can see the future."

Julian stared at her blankly for a moment, before his eyes widened. "You want me to tap in on Cromfield? The guy's hundreds of years old. I don't know if I can even—"

"You need to try," Rae said firmly, squeezing his wrist. "People's lives depend on it, Jules."

He stared at her for another second, before he nodded shakily and closed his eyes. "I'll try...I just don't really know what to focus on. I've never met him. He's, like, a historical figure."

This time it was Devon who took over. He seemed almost relieved to be doing so. Coaching his friend through the maze of his visions was something normal, something he could latch on to. "You don't need to know him personally; you know he's alive. You know he's out there. Just focus on the man in the picture. Get inside his head..."

Julian breathed deeply as his face tightened in concentration. For a moment, nothing happened. Then, all at once, his eyes shot open at the speed of light.

There was no color in them—they were painted in an iridescent, glassy shade of white. It would have been a startling sight, especially set against his dark hair in the shadowed car, but his friends had seen it happen so many times, they were almost immune.

That being said, this vision seemed to be a bit different than the others.

"Jules?" Devon leaned forward suddenly, shaking his shoulders. "You okay, mate?"

Instead of his usual blank expression, there was a distinct grimace on his face, a look that made it clear he was in pain. He had braced himself against the car, but was leaning back slightly, almost as if he was trying to fight his way out of something. After a tense moment, a thin stream of blood trickled from his nose.

"Julian!" Devon shook him again.

Julian stayed in his trance for another second, but then suddenly awoke with a gasp. He stared around the car in disorientation, before lifting his hand to his bloody nose in surprise.

"You alright?" Molly exclaimed, her skin significantly paler than usual.

For a second, Julian didn't look so sure, but then his face cleared and he nodded quickly. "Yeah, I'm fine. That was just..." He shook his head. "I'm fine." His dark eyes snapped up to Rae. "I know where he's going first. We're going to need to pack some clothes. It'll be a bit of a trip."

In a flash, Molly hopped out of the car, pulling Julian out with her. "I'll pack a suitcase for me and Rae, and Julian can get some stuff for him and Devon. You guys just hang tight here," she instructed, eyeing Rae with concern. "We'll meet you back here as fast as we can."

Before anyone could answer, she'd taken off into the dark, pulling Julian along behind her.

No one noticed them as they slipped past the hordes of partiers wandering the school grounds. Devon and Rae watched intently as they parted in the middle of the lawn and took off in opposite directions—Molly heading to Aumbry House and Julian to Joist Hall. A second later, they had vanished completely.

For the first time all night, Rae leaned back in her seat with a bit of relief. Sometimes, it helped to have a best friend who knew her emotions as well as Rae knew them herself. She didn't want to be anywhere near her schoolmates right now. She didn't want to risk running into her mom, she didn't want to be on school grounds; to be honest, she didn't even really want to talk to Devon.

But it seemed there was no avoiding that one. After her little stunt with the truck, Molly was obviously hesitant to leave her alone.

Rae sighed and angled herself so she was staring back out the window, avoiding Devon's worried eyes. She hadn't meant anything by the truck. At some level, she knew it wouldn't kill her. But it was like she just had to prove it to the rest of herself, to her waking brain, that simply couldn't process the fact that she was going to be walking around as a teenager in London of 2099.

In a way, that same warped part of her that needed proof with the truck was almost relieved. At least now she had answers, no matter how terrible they were. This was why everyone looked older in their school pictures, but she looked exactly the same. Maybe this was even why she had grown up outside the world of tatùs. She was never meant to be around them for very long, was she? Sure, she'd get to know a generation or two, but then they'd age out and die, and she'd have to latch on to the next one. That is, if she wanted to keep latching on at all. Somehow, she doubted it. Who would willingly latch on to wave after wave of people, only to have them ripped away? Who could stand living with such loss?

Well...I'll have to stand it, she thought with a dark clarity. *My entire life is going to revolve around loss. That's the nature of all things permanent, isn't it? No home, no friends, no family, no—*

"Rae?"

She jumped guiltily in her seat and cast a backwards glance at Devon. "Yeah?"

His eyes swept briefly over her face, for one of the first times unsure as to what to say to her. "Do you want to...? Shouldn't we talk about what's going on? I mean...what you found in in Cromfield's letter—"

"There's more important stuff going on right now," she said swiftly, shutting down the subject before it could even begin. What good would talking do? They could talk about it forever and it wouldn't change anything. Well, *she* could talk about it forever...

He slid closer towards her on the seat. "Honey...we *are* going to find a way through this. You don't need to keep it all to yourself. There has to be a way we can—"

"Devon, I really don't want to talk about this now, okay?" Nervously, she tucked her hair behind her ears as she tried to stem the wave of nerves eating away at her stomach. "I hear what you're saying, and I appreciate it, but right now we have a list of people to save. That's what I want to focus on, okay? The other stuff," she waved her hand as if trying to dismiss it, "I can't handle right now."

He nodded seriously, taking her hand. "Okay, that's fine. Just know, whenever you do want to talk about it, I'm here, alright?"

She nodded briskly and turned her face away before he could see the tears.

She wanted to talk about it, alright. Of course she wanted to talk about it. In fact, she wanted to tear her hair out and scream bloody murder at the stormy sky. But there simply wasn't time. And, under the circumstances, that was probably a good thing.

She didn't need more time; she needed a distraction—something to steady her shaking hands. And if that distraction happened to be saving the world of hybrids from a psychopathic madman bent on global domination?

That would have to do. For now.

Chapter 2

"Here you are, Flight 267 to Puerto Suárez." An airline receptionist half-hidden beneath a virtual helmet of chemically-drenched hair, looked up at Devon with a dreamy smile. "And what class will you be flying?"

Now that the wave of adrenaline they had ridden to the airport had started to fade, Rae stared in open, exhausted astonishment at the woman's carefully sculpted coiffeur. She had never seen so much hairspray on one person before. Was it hard to the touch? Like cardboard? It looked like, if she tapped her knuckles against it, it might make a sound...

Julian and Molly hovered anxiously behind as Devon pulled a credit card from his wallet. But Rae, unable to process how her entire world had turned upside-down in less than twenty-four hours, latched onto one insignificant detail with a vengeance.

Maybe Molly shouldn't be standing so close, she thought to herself, staring with wide eyes. *One misplaced spark and the woman's whole head could go up in smoke...*

She tuned back in to hear Devon say, "It doesn't matter, as long as we're all together."

Molly cleared her throat sharply behind him, and he rolled his eyes.

"On second thought, if you had something up in first-class, that would be great."

The woman quickly printed off their boarding passes, scribbling what looked suspiciously like her phone number on Devon's receipt, and the four of them headed off to customs.

When Julian had said 'a bit of a trip,' he'd meant the rural countryside in the heart of Bolivia. Rae shook her head as she glanced around the crowded airport. Her psychic friend had always had a rather loose grasp on geographical scale. *Bolivia*. She should have known.

She tightened the straps on her backpack and joined her friends in the seemingly endless line to get through security. All around them, dozens of happy, carefree teenagers were reuniting with their families. Guilder's graduation coincided with most of the other London schools, and the airport was packed with kids either heading home, or, more often, kids flying back to England for the summer holiday.

Rae watched as a girl about her age barreled down the corridor and jumped into the arms of her waiting father. The pair looked remarkably alike. Both tall, with waves of wispy blond hair, and both of them closed their eyes at the exact same moment when they smiled. A second later, he picked up her bags and they headed out to the parking lot, chattering away in matching Cockney accents.

It took Rae a minute to realize she wasn't the only one watching.

Apparently Devon was having an emotional roller-coaster all of his own. His bright eyes fixed on the same pair she'd been observing, before wandering to another family behind them. This time, it was a father and son who shook hands briefly before the father pulled the boy in for a fierce embrace.

Devon's face tightened for a moment before he turned deliberately away. It was then that Rae suddenly remembered her talk with Devon's father, Dean Wardell, just the previous evening. So much had happened since then that she'd put it entirely from her mind, assuming that the Dean would simply speak to Devon himself when they returned to Guilder.

Except they weren't going back to Guilder. In fact, with the number of names on the list, they had no realistic idea of when they'd be returning. Instead of celebrating the summer holidays like the rest of their friends, instead of leaping into the waiting arms of their own parents and heading home, they were off to Bolivia to find a boy whose name had been placed on a psychopath's hit list.

Just your average summer vacation.

"Your dad talked to me after graduation," Rae blurted suddenly, speaking in a voice so soft only Devon would be able to hear.

He turned to her in surprise. "He did?" His face suddenly tensed in preemptive anger. "Rae, whatever he told you, just ignore it. He has no say, alright? This is *my* life. It's *our* relationship. He can throw me out on the streets if he wants to, but that's never going to change. And if he thinks—"

"He gave us his blessing."

Devon stopped short as the words hung in the air between them. Seeing his blank look of surprise, Rae couldn't help but smile; a smile which soon darkened with faint traces of suppressed hysteria as she realized the ironic timing of the blessed event.

Of course the Dean would decide to condone their relationship *now*. A mere twenty-four hours before Rae found out she was cursed to live forever, so any kind of 'future' with Devon would be tragically one-sided. She wondered if Devon was putting two and two together yet. How the chance of a never-ending life for only one of them essentially doomed a shared life for both of them.

On the upside, Uncle Argyle was sure to be thrilled.

"He..." Devon seemed to be having a hard time saying the words. "He gave us his *blessing*?"

By then, Julian and Molly had turned to them in interest.

"Who did?" Molly asked. "Your *dad*? That's amazing, Dev!"

Julian smiled. "Does that mean you can stop sleeping on my couch? Not to rush you," he added quickly, "but I'd love to get a full night's sleep without waking up to hear you and Rae texting each other at four in the morning. Some people are not night owls, and need their sleep."

Devon ignored both of them and focused completely on Rae, still unable to imagine a scenario in which his father would ever relent. "What did he say, exactly?"

Rae shelved her darker feelings for the time being and tried to smile. "He said your happiness was the most important thing in the world to him. That he was only trying to protect you, but he realized he had been wrong. He said he'd do whatever he had to make it right."

Devon was clearly stunned. He moved up in line to the metal detectors like he was floating rather than walking, his thoughts a million miles away as he knelt down and began taking off his shoes.

"Sir, do you have any liquids or electronics in your bag?" a nameless security guard barked routinely. "If you do, you need to remove them at this time."

All at once, Devon's trance was broken as he and Julian shared a panicked look.

"I didn't even think..." Julian muttered, turning pale.

Devon's eyes grew wide. "This isn't a sanctioned mission."

"What's going on?" Rae stared back and forth at the two boys.

"It's not PC security," Devon hissed in a hushed tone.

"What're you guys talking about?" Molly asked impatiently, glancing at the restless line of people waiting behind them.

Devon looked abruptly uncomfortable. "We may have some things that might not exactly pass a customs check."

Rae folded her arms across her chest, shooting the security guard an innocent smile. "Like what? You guys smuggling in kiwis or something?" she murmured between clenched teeth.

The boys exchanged another look.

"A couple knives..."

"Maybe a Taser or two."

"There's that pair of brass knuckles I got in Mexico."

"Some Vitamin Water."

The back and forth stopped abruptly, and the girls turned in unison to Julian as he tagged that last one on at the end. He caught their disbelieving smiles and threw up his hands defensively. "Okay, so the water isn't that bad, but we're not allowed to have any liquids, are we?" he snapped.

Rae stifled a grin then turned to Devon. "Why the hell are you carrying a knife?"

He raised his eyebrows. "You think I was going to break into a church to track down a five-hundred-year-old psycho without arming myself first?"

"Yeah, but a *knife*?"

"After Kraigan pulled a gun on us in the parking lot? Yeah—a knife, Rae. Remember, not all of us can turn invisible."

Molly turned to a bewildered couple standing behind them and smiled sweetly. "They're rehearsing for a play..."

"Look, it doesn't matter," Rae said quickly. "You guys run to the bathroom or something and throw all that stuff away. We'll meet you at the gate."

"What?" Julian complained. "Rae, it's expensive stuff."

"These PC Tasers aren't so easy to replace," Devon added sullenly.

Rae threw up her hands, shooting the security guard another apologetic look. "What do you guys want me to say? You prefer getting arrested by airport security because you won't ditch your super-spy throwing stars, be my guest." She turned in a huff to Molly. "You didn't pack anything weird in *my* bag, did you?"

Molly shook her head dismissively. "Some super-cute stockings I know you'll wrongfully hate, but other than that, no. But, Rae, aren't you forgetting something?"

Rae shook her head. "What?"

"Cassidy's tatù." Molly smiled. "Devon was right. You can literally turn invisible now. I'm sure you can find a way to get us through customs undetected..."

"That was so unbelievably cool." Devon grinned smugly as he kicked back in his seat.

Thirty minutes later, he and Rae were sitting in the first-class passenger's lounge waiting to board their flight, having just dropped out of the security line and then doubled back through it, jumping the barrier while holding hands in an invisible line.

"I can't believe you were able to expand the cloak to include the rest of us," he continued, looking at Rae with unmistakable pride. "Cassidy will want you to show her that one for sure."

"We're just lucky it worked," Rae sighed, running her hands back through her hair. "What if it had worn off halfway through? How would Carter and his band of government cronies have bailed us out of that?"

That was the last thing they needed at this point: For Carter and the rest of the Privy Council, not to mention, Rae's own *mother*, to find out what they were up to.

Devon gave her a cocky smirk. "They'd have found a way. And Julian would have seen if it wasn't going to work."

Rae swiveled around in her chair to stare through the terminal. "Speaking of Julian, where is he? He and Molly were supposed to be back fifteen minutes ago."

Devon glanced up with a bland smile. "Not sure about Molly, but if I had to guess about Julian, I'd say he's accessorizing."

As if on cue, Rae spotted a head of dark hair with a ponytail winding its way through the crowd. A second later, Julian pushed open the door to the lounge to join them—sporting a pair of some of the biggest, blackest sunglasses Rae had ever seen. She blinked up at him as he took a seat beside her, frowning with concern. "Jules, I say this as a friend, you need to stop taking the Matrix so seriously."

Devon snickered while Julian swatted her with his boarding pass. "It's my freaking eyes," he muttered. "I can never tell when they're going to white-out and send a flight attendant running for the hills. Besides, we still need to know exactly where in Bolivia Cromfield is heading." He sank down in his chair with a tired sigh. "I'm afraid I have some work to do..."

Rae's eyes tightened as she watched him rest his head bracingly on the chair. The last time Julian tapped into Cromfield's mind had been very different from any of his other visions. Instead of acting as an unobtrusive observer, it had almost looked as though he was getting pulled in against his will, fighting off a mental assault.

Yes, they needed the information. But *no*, she wasn't willing to put one of her friends on the chopping block just to find an address. They could always go through the proper channels. "Julian, are you sure you—"

But at that moment, Molly collapsed in the little space between them, dropping several bags of airport purchases at their feet. When Molly stressed, she shopped. Then again, she tended to shop regardless, so if was often hard to tell. Both Julian and Rae scooted over automatically to make room, highly accustomed to such behavior, as the little redhead whipped out her phone and began texting at the speed of light, completely oblivious to the intrusion.

But while Rae just rolled her eyes and looked away, Devon was watching Molly with a serious expression on his handsome face. His eyes flicked to her phone before he shifted casually forward in his seat. "Who are you texting, Molls?" he asked innocently.

"What?" She glanced up before returning to the screen. "Oh, Luke. I was just letting him know where we were going and— *HEY!*"

Faster than sight, Devon snatched the phone from her hands and crushed it silently in his own. Rae watched the little shards of metal fall to the ground in shock, her mouth falling open as she both stared at Devon and discreetly held back her infuriated friend.

"What the hell did you do that for, Wardell?!" Molly demanded in a rage.

Tiny, almost imperceptible sparks began dancing at the tips of her fingers, and Rae took her firmly by the hands, glancing nervously around the crowded lounge.

"They're going to be looking for us," Devon said quietly, wiping the metallic dust discreetly onto his pants. "I'm sorry, Molls, but none of us can use our phones anymore. It's not safe."

Her eyes flashed dangerously as she leaned across Rae. "It was *Luke*, Devon. It's not like he's going to tell—"

"Every call can be traced," he interrupted with only a thin layer of patience. "Every text. The second we don't come back to Guilder; we're going to be at the top of the PC's watch list. Everyone we know will be put under surveillance. Even Luke."

Molly slumped back against her chair in a huff. "Well, you didn't have to break it. You could have just taken out the memory card or something—"

"That wouldn't have worked." Devon seemed just as frustrated as she was to have to be explaining such basic agency tricks. "Molls, you haven't really been out in the field; you're going to need to trust—"

"Oh, that's what this whole thing is about?" she interrupted furiously. "I'm out here with the rest of you, volunteering to run all over the world, risking my life to find this lunatic, but because I haven't been on as many agency-sanctioned missions as you've been, it's suddenly not good enough—"

"That's not what I'm saying—"

"Now boarding Flight 267 to Puerto Suárez. Calling all first-class passengers at this time..."

Saved by the bell, Rae thought as she hoisted on her backpack. She glanced back at the others as she got to her feet, but Julian was lost in a trance, and Molly and Devon were still glaring at each other, arms folded tightly over their chests. Fortunately, none of the other people in the lounge seemed to have noticed the little dispute when it happened, but they were certainly noticing now, casting curious looks at the group of beautiful, angry-looking teenagers as they filed past.

"Come on, guys," Rae reasoned softly, positioning herself cautiously in between them. "Let's not do this now. We don't have the time, and we're attracting attention." Neither one moved, and she sighed, wishing she had some sort of tatù that could calm tempers. "Molly," she glanced sympathetically at her friend, "he'll buy you a new phone when we get back."

"The second we get to London," Devon promised.

There wasn't much apology in his voice, but they glanced stiffly at each other, and a tentative truce was made.

Rolling her eyes, Molly pushed to her feet. She kicked Julian awake, muttering, "Whenever *that* will be..."

Nonetheless, she picked up her purse and headed off to the gate, leaving Devon to carry her many bags as penance. Julian trailed along behind, half in the present, half in the future, while Rae brought up the rear, watching them closely.

It wasn't like her friends to argue, let alone in public, and it certainly wasn't like them to get careless and slip into their tatùs. If they didn't start being careful, they'd have more than just the Privy Council on their trail...

Once they got on the plane, things weren't much better.

Julian immediately put on his sunglasses and fell into a silent trance, desperately trying to see where to go once they landed. Molly started downing little bottles of complimentary champagne like they were going out of style. And Devon...

While Devon seemed fine on the outside, Rae knew better. After all these years, she was able to read his moods almost as well as her own. He was just barely keeping it together, maintaining a carefully neutral expression, while inside, he was spinning out of control.

That's when Rae realized that just because her friends hadn't received the same life-altering news she had didn't mean they weren't just as traumatized by what had happened. They'd all been down in the catacombs, too. They'd all see the same gruesome pictures. The same bloody threats.

And they'd all decided to come along on this wild goose-chase without a second's thought.

Suddenly, the quick tempers and little bottles of booze made sense. She wasn't the only one hanging on by a thread; she wasn't the only one wishing she was one of those kids in the airport, or one of the kids still partying it up at Guilder. She wasn't the only one who wanted to go home to a carefree summer with her family, not have the weight of the world on her shoulders for once.

Get a grip, Rae. Pull it together for your friends.

"Hey." She squeezed Devon's leg, fixing a determined smile on her face. "You know when we get to Bolivia, I'm going to get to use Sarah's tatù for the first time."

The future Queen of England, with whom Rae had recently struck an unlikely friendship, had the useful ability of being able to speak and understand any language on the planet. Quite handy considering she was going into professional politics, but Rae had yet to test it out.

Devon glanced over at her in surprise before smiling tentatively himself. "I hate to break it to you, babe, but both Julian and I speak Spanish quite fluently."

"Oh..." Rae paused, feeling rather deflated, before suddenly rallying, "Well, that may be, but can you also translate any of the fifty indigenous dialects we may run across in some of the smaller villages?" She grinned victoriously at his blank expression. "Yeah. I didn't think so."

For a second, he just stared at her in bewilderment—probably wondering where this sudden bout of playful energy came from. Then he angled towards her in his chair with a bemused smile.

"Are you tatù-shaming me?" he asked incredulously.

"Oh no," she said with mock seriousness. "I would never presume that one tatù—and thus—one person, was superior to another. But if the shoe fits..."

His eyebrows shot up and he grinned for real, his nervous energy temporarily forgotten as his competitive streak rose to the surface. "Is that right? Well I'll have you know, Kerrigan, I learned to speak four different languages all on my own. I didn't need some fancy tatù to do it for me."

"*Four?*" Rae patted his hand indulgently. "Aw, honey, that is so cute."

"Shut up," he chuckled, turning back to the front.

Satisfied that at least one person was temporarily back on the straight and narrow, Rae leaned across him to deal with Molly. By now there was a little graveyard of empty bottles around her, and she was hiccupping nervously as she stared out the window. Occasionally, she would reach automatically for her phone, and then glare at Devon when she remembered it wasn't there.

"Hey, Molls?" Rae tossed a copy of Sky Mall across the aisle. "I was thinking we could take some of this time to start accessorizing our new apartment. It is a thirteen-hour flight, you know..."

Molly's eyes dilated slightly as she caught the magazine mid-spin. Thirteen hours of non-interrupted shopping? Perhaps there was hope for the day after all...

"Rae, that's—" she hiccupped, "brilliant!"

Rae grinned as Molly started flipping through the pages, leaning back in her chair with a satisfied expression on her face. Julian was out cold, but she was sure she could think of something for him later. In the meantime, balance had been at least momentarily restored.

"Bet you think you're pretty sneaky, don't you?" Devon teased.

Rae glanced up with a guilty grin. Sometimes she forgot that Devon knew her just as well as she knew him.

"Yeah, well," she sighed and curled into him, "it's been a tough day all around."

He kissed the top of her forehead and wrapped his arm around her shoulders. "It certainly has." They were quiet for a while before he said, "I saw you left *your* phone in Julian's car. Are you worried about what your mom's gonna do when she finds out you're gone?"

Rae's throat tightened as she considered it for the millionth time. What was her mom going to do? She was going to freak the hell out. That's exactly what she was going to do. "She knows this whole year we've been working towards finding Cromfield..." she said half-heartedly. "I guess I can only hope she'll trust that we know what we're doing."

Devon paused for a second. "Do we?"

Rae glanced up and met his eyes. "It's best we don't overthink that part."

They chuckled softly as the plane revved its engines and began streaking down the runway. A moment later, they were above the clouds.

"Get some sleep, love," Devon murmured. "We're going to have a long day tomorrow."

Rae shut her eyes and rested her head against his chest.

He was right about that. It was going to be a long day.

The first of many.

Chapter 3

"Sir? Sir, are you alright? You need to fasten your seatbelt for landing. *Sir?*"

Rae opened her eyes to see a rather concerned-looking flight attendant hovering over Julian's chair. Jules was still out cold, locked in his visions, and essentially dead to the world. On his other side, Molly lay drooling against the window, sleeping off the booze.

"Devon," Rae whispered anxiously, prodding him awake.

His eyes snapped open at once and instantly followed her gaze across the aisle. Using perhaps a bit more speed than was wise, he leapt to his feet, catching the attendant's wrist as she reached worriedly for Julian's sunglasses.

She startled in fright, but he flashed her an easy smile. "My friend suffers from narcolepsy," he lied with surprising confidence, kneeling down and fastening Julian's seatbelt for him. Watching the practiced movements, Rae got the feeling he had done this before. "But thank you for your concern. I can take it from here."

Though the woman was easily three times Devon's age, she blushed to the roots of her teased-up hair and gently squeezed his shoulder. "That's very good of you, young man," she purred, batting her thick eyelashes. "Be sure to take your seat as soon as you can for landing."

Devon smiled and pulled himself politely away. "Yes, ma'am."

As the woman vanished toward the cockpit, Rae cleared her throat loudly, her eyes dancing with amusement as she grinned at her blushing boyfriend. As the Privy Council usually paired Devon up with Julian for this sort of thing, she hardly ever got to see this hilariously persecuted side of him. She thought back to the airline receptionist scribbling her phone number on the back of his ticket receipt. Did this kind of thing happen all the time?

Devon, for one, seemed incredibly reluctant to meet her eyes, focusing instead on Julian. "Jules," he muttered, shaking his shoulders discreetly, "wake up!"

Julian stayed frozen as a statue, eyes an iridescent white beneath the glasses, lost in the future.

Devon tried again, shaking him more roughly this time. "Julian—*wake up*! Come on, man, open your eyes."

Still nothing. Even drooling Molly started to stir.

Devon glanced back at Rae and sighed. "It's getting harder and harder to wake him. I've had to carry him out before. And now that he's watching Cromfield..." He tutted and turned back to his friend with concern. "I've never seen him out this long before."

"Try Molly," Rae advised. "She can wake him."

Unfortunately, as Molly's roommate when they were both coming into their powers, Rae had been the victim of the 'Molly Skye Morning Wakeup' many times herself. She knew firsthand how effective it was.

With a grin, Devon poked the half-sleeping girl in her side. "Morning, sunshine!"

In a blur of crimson hair, Molly jerked awake, spluttering, "Cash or credit?!" When she saw her friends watching with incredulous smiles, she gathered herself together as dignifiedly as she could.

"Trapped in the world of retail again?" Rae asked knowingly. Molly rarely had nightmares, but they all seemed to center around the same thing.

Molly shuddered, pulling her coat tighter up around her. "I was wearing polyester."

Devon made a commendable effort not to roll his eyes. "Molls, do you think you could wake Julian for us? I can't get him out of this vision, and we're about to land..."

"Yeah, sure." She yawned and stretched. Then, with hardly a glance, she reached over and zapped Julian discreetly in the side, sending a few volts of electricity coursing through his body.

His eyes shot open with a gasp as he jumped in his seat, falling back when he hit the leather restraint.

"And that's why we always wear our seatbelts," Devon teased lightly. He clapped his friend on the shoulder, his eyes taking in every minute detail though he kept his face free of concern. "Are you okay? You were out for a while there."

Julian glanced around, clearly disoriented, before his eyes struggled to focus on Devon. "I don't..." He took a deep breath and squeezed his hands into fists. "Yeah, I think so."

Rae bit her lip, climbing out of her chair and kneeling next to Devon in the aisle. "Your nose is bleeding again," she said softly. Julian's hand came up to his face as she and Devon shared a worried glance. "Jules, I know I said we needed your tat—ability, but not at your expense." She caught herself just in time, not sure who might be listening. She lowered her voice, "You *just* got a handle on these more intense visions of yours. Maybe you shouldn't be pushing it with Cromfield—"

"Don't be silly." He wiped his face clean and gave her a reassuring wink. "I'm fine. And besides...I now know the name of the village where Cromfield is heading."

"*Excuse me*," the sharp voice of the same flight attendant who'd been melting over Devon interrupted their conversation, "you *all* need to return to your seats now." She seemed considerably less taken with him now that her eyes fell critically on Rae kneeling by his side. She did, however, pat Julian comfortingly on the arm before she left. "You just hang in there, sweetie. We're landing soon."

Julian's dark eyes shot up in confusion, as Rae and Devon, both fighting smiles, retreated across the aisle and buckled in for landing.

The second they stepped outside, the hot Bolivian sun hit them like a slap to the face. Not only was it hotter, but it was also more humid than anything Rae had ever experienced before. The air felt thick, like a turtleneck around her throat. She gulped a couple of deep breaths, feeling a bit like she was drowning, before dropping her bags in defeat on the sidewalk. The formfitting black spy gear the four of them were still wearing from the church wasn't helping things, and, already, she could feel her hair sticking to the back of her neck. She envisioned curls and ringlets forming from her straightened hair. "Well, this is just lovely!" She took off her heavy London coat and stuffed it into the nearest bag. "Really fits the climate."

Molly smacked her shoulder with a grin. "Hey—I packed the best I could, alright? It's not like any of us really had a South American wardrobe."

Devon was all business, running his fingers back through his suddenly damp hair as he hailed a taxi. "First things first: Jules, you said it was to the north?"

Julian nodded thoughtfully. "It's a little farming village right on the border. There should be a hotel nearby. We can stay there for the night after we find the kid."

"The *kid*?" Molly asked in surprise. "How do you know he's a *kid*?"

He was about to answer, but, at that moment, a cab pulled up to the sidewalk and the four of them climbed inside, rolling down the windows to try to create a little breeze. Devon muttered some instructions to the driver, and, a second later, they were flying up the street, merging onto some kind of interstate.

Once they were safely on their way, and it was clear the driver was no longer paying attention to them, Molly lowered her voice and asked again, "So...how do you know he's a kid? I guess I kind of pictured him as our age."

Julian shook his head. "Cromfield's files on all the hybrids were more extensive than just what we found at the church. I saw the kid in his mind. He's only about seven or eight. I don't think he even knows he's going to have powers yet. He's still years away from getting his tatù."

"Well, then this can be a nice little surprise for him," Rae murmured as she gazed out the window at the Bolivian countryside.

For whatever reason, she had pictured all the hybrids as teenagers as well. It was just easier to think of them as being already tatùed and in some way capable of defending themselves. She hadn't imagined that some of the names on the list might be children.

The four of them were silent for the rest of the two-hour drive. Julian caught up on some of the sleep he'd missed on the plane, Molly stared out the window, nervously chewing her lip, while Rae and Devon simply held hands, both quietly thinking about what was to come.

The problem that worried them all was that this wasn't an agency-sanctioned mission. They had no team, there was no official plan. All they knew was they had to get to each of the hybrids on the list before Cromfield did, but after that...?

They hadn't quite worked it out yet.

When they finally pulled into the little town, the afternoon sun was high in the sky, shining down unforgivingly as they scuttled under the eaves to what looked to be the hotel. Armed with her new tatù, curtesy of the future Queen of England, Rae headed up to the front desk and secured them three rooms before getting directions to the local elementary school. Apparently, most Bolivian schools still had another two weeks before letting out for the summer, and if the child was as young as Julian said, he would most likely still be there at this time of day.

"What're we going to do if we find Cromfield?" Molly asked quietly as they made their way down the street to the school.

It was an obvious question each of them had deliberately avoided asking, but now that the moment had come upon them, something had to be said. The problem? This obvious question begged question of its own: Cromfield was a man with two non-violent tatùs. How the hell had he managed to capture, subdue, and kill over a hundred powerful hybrids with tatùs of their own?

It didn't add up. It didn't make sense. And it sent chills of fear down Rae's spine. Down all their spines.

They were missing some key component. Something critical that had turned Cromfield from a crazed lunatic to an actual serial killer. And until they knew that that thing was, they were going to have to try to avoid him at all costs.

Not an easy feat, considering they were the uninvited guests on his international road trip.

"If we see him, you all run." Rae glanced at Molly's doubtful face and patted her reassuringly on the back. "In the meantime, we'll just try to blend in..."

Molly glanced down at their sweltering black spy gear and gulped. "Blend in. Sure..."

They weren't nearly as inconspicuous as any of them would have liked, but the locals were friendly enough, smiling, but generally ignoring them as they made their way down the street to the school.

The bell had just rung, releasing the kids for the day, and the four friends watched silently as a swarm of them poured out onto the grass as they made their way home.

"That's him," Julian said suddenly as they stared through the chain-link fence. He pointed to a little boy with a mop of brown curls leapfrogging across the jungle gym.

Rae's breath caught in her chest. Julian was right. He couldn't have been any older than seven. His sparkling eyes and rosy cheeks reminded her of those little porcelain statues of cherubim that stores started selling around Christmas. When his tinkling laugh rang out suddenly across the grass, her eyes welled with unwanted tears and her fingers wrapped around the fence.

This kid was innocent. Blameless.

And somehow—on Cromfield's list.

All because he was like her. Innocent, and marked a victim.

As the swarm of kids marched past the fence, the boy paused curiously, as did the rest of the students, gazing up at the four strangers in their strange clothes. Judging by the whispers and looks of open astonishment, their little village must not get visitors very often. Nonetheless, the boy skipped trustingly forward when Rae smiled and waved to him.

"Hola," she said with forced cheerfulness, looking him up and down, "Estás Matti Padron?"

"Sí," he answered excitedly, bouncing from foot to foot, clearly pleased with all the attention. "I speak English," he continued with a faint note of pride.

Are we that obvious?

Rae grinned encouragingly. "Matti, my name's Rae and these are my friends." The three of them waved awkwardly behind her. "We came all the way from England to talk to you and your parents. Do you think we could walk you home?"

With the unquestioning obedience of a child, Matti nodded and waved them on, slipping his hand automatically into Rae's as they crossed the street. She smiled to herself and gave it a little squeeze as a whole flood of conflicting emotions came welling up inside her.

How trusting he was. How sweet!

How easy it would be for Cromfield to make off with him.

Matti lived with his parents in a tiny house on the edge of town. After Devon quickly checked the perimeter, and Julian just as quickly checked the future for any immediate problems, the four of them knocked on the door, with the child standing front and center.

It was difficult to say who looked more surprised—the mother or the father.

"Can I help you?" Mrs. Padron asked nervously in broken English, her eyes widening as she stared at the four strangers surrounding her son. The next second, she snapped her fingers, and the boy ran to her side, wedging himself in between his parents with a grin.

"Mr. and Mrs. Padron?" Rae asked cautiously, keeping her distance so as not to alarm them any further.

The couple shared a bewildered glance before the man nodded. "Yes?"

Great, Rae thought to herself, *now what?*

Should she just lift up her shirt, show them her ink, and ask if she could come inside?

Surprisingly enough, it was Molly who stepped suddenly forward. She eyed Mr. Padron curiously before slowly extending her hand. After a moment's hesitation, he leaned forward to shake it. But before he could, a bunch of sparks came flying out from her fingertips, and he jumped back.

"Molly!" Rae reprimanded, elbowing her furiously in the side.

But Mr. Padron was staring at her as if gazing at his own reflection. A strange look came over his face, and, the next second, a shower of sparks shot from his hand as well.

"I knew it." Molly smiled. "It's very nice to meet you both."

Mrs. Padron gaped at her before turning her attention back to Rae. "You can...you can do what we can do?" She sounded absolutely shocked, but there was something else in her voice, too.

Excitement.

For whatever reason, the words sent a feeling of deep relief radiating through Rae's entire body, and she flashed a genuine smile. "Yes, we can."

Then her eyes fell on Matti, who was still grinning excitedly up at Molly like he was hoping for more sparks.

"But there's more," she said hesitantly, almost unwilling to continue. "We came here to talk to you about your son. He's in danger."

"So this man...he's coming here?"

Matti had been sent outside to play in the garden, and a plate of cookies sat untouched on the kitchen table before the four of them and Matti's parents.

"Yes," Rae said quietly, "he's coming here."

The Padrons shared a quick look before gazing out the window at their son. The father asked, "And you know this for sure?"

Rae nodded gently, her heart breaking for them. "My friend," she gestured to Julian, "can see the future. He saw the man was on his way. He wants your son. Matti's name is on his list."

She realized she was unconsciously avoiding saying Cromfield's name, as if saying it might bring him here sooner. Throughout the entire story, the Padrons had listened curiously, not realizing how it all connected to them. But now that they'd come to the end, a chill had fallen over the sunny little kitchen.

All was quiet for a moment before Mr. Padron suddenly slammed his hands down on the table, sending a spray of sparks flying into the air. "Let him come! Theresa and I aren't afraid. We can protect our son."

Rae bowed her head. She understood the sentiment entirely. But facts were facts. If Cromfield was to come here, the Padrons wouldn't stand a chance. And neither would Matti.

"Mr. Padron," Devon began peaceably, "I know exactly how you feel." His eyes flickered to Rae, and she felt herself blush. "I promise you, there's *nothing* I would rather do than tear the man from limb from limb," he took a breath to steady himself, "but that's simply not possible. Until we know how he's doing what he's doing, the best thing you can do to protect your family is hide."

"*Hide*?!" Mr. Padron's eyes flashed. "This is my son we're talking about. How can you expect us to—"

A scream echoed in the little kitchen as Rae suddenly caught on fire.

The Padrons shouted and jumped back, while Molly rolled her eyes and muttered something that sounded like, 'show-off.'

Outside, little Matti ran to the window and stared in open-mouthed amazement. Rae stood there for a second, letting the message sink in, before dousing the flames.

"That's what I can do." She stared Mr. Padron intently in the eyes. "And *I'm* hiding from him."

A few hours later, the four friends were heading back down the street to the hotel. They had planned to leave much sooner, but Mrs. Padron had insisted on feeding them dinner while her husband hastily packed their bags. As impressed as she'd been with their little performance, she said they were still kids themselves and she couldn't, in good conscience, let them walk away hungry.

As per Rae's instructions, the little family was leaving the village that night. As of yet, they weren't sure where they were going to go; they would simply head to the bus station and decide when they got there. Julian had tried to explain it as best he could. Make split-second decisions. Try to avoid making plans.

The more fluid everything was, the harder time Cromfield would have tracking them.

Unfortunately, the same rules applied to the four of them.

"Well, if we weren't on Cromfield's radar before, we definitely are now," Molly murmured as they pushed open the door to the hotel and headed through the lobby to the lounge. It was dimly-lit and they were apparently the only visitors in town, so the four of them settled into a corner booth and talked without fear of being overheard.

Julian's face tightened as he traced his fingers in a groove on the table. "I think I'm already on his radar."

Devon head shot up in alarm. "What do you mean? There's no way he can know if you're watching him, Jules. It doesn't work like that."

Julian nodded distractedly but turned with sudden interest to Molly. "How did you know that Mr. Padron had your same tatù?"

Rae leaned forward curiously. She had been wondering the same thing.

Molly answered with a little shrug. "I could just...tell. I don't know how to explain it, but it's like we had some kind of connection. I noticed the same thing with Noah when I was mentoring him back at school." She glanced up at Rae. "Have you ever had something like that? I mean, you have so many abilities..."

Rae frowned as she considered it. "I'm not sure. Not really, but maybe that's just because, while I might be sharing other people's tatùs, no one I know has mine. Maybe it would be different if I met another mimic." She shook her head. "I might have felt it with Kraigan. Not at first, but maybe I did. I don't know."

"Why do you ask?" Devon asked Julian sharply. "Are you saying that—"

"I'm not saying anything," Julian said quickly, pushing to his feet. He ran his hands through his long hair before securing it in its customary ponytail. "I'm going up to bed. I need to try to get another vision as to where we should go next." He sighed, sounded older than his years. "Goodnight, you guys."

"Goodnight," Molly called back to him, and Devon nodded, but Rae watched him go with a frown.

"Do you think...we should be letting him do that anymore?" she asked warily.

Devon sighed. "No. I don't. But I also don't see what choice we have." Molly and Rae glanced at him curiously and he shook his head, looking abruptly tired. "Can you imagine what might have happened if we'd taken the time to go through the government channels to find Matti?"

Rae shuddered as she watched her friend climb the stairs into the dark.

No. She didn't want to imagine that for one second.

Chapter 4

Purgatory.

Rae had never given it much thought, the concept of being trapped in torturous limbo for some undetermined amount of time. It wasn't an idea she'd been raised with, and she could honesty say that it had probably never crossed her mind.

Well, it sure as hell did now.

"Just look at the list again," Devon said with increasingly strained patience. "Look at it again, and really focus this time, Julian."

Julian slapped his hands down on the table and pushed back his chair. "Look at the list again? Why not?" He shook his head. "Only because I've been staring at the damn thing for the last, oh, I don't know, *six hours.*"

"Guys, this isn't—" Rae tried to interject.

"I know you're frustrated, but you need to try to focus!" Devon looked like Carter as his finger tapped against the list.

"Focus? What the hell do you think I've been doing this whole time?" Julian's voice rose as he stood. "You think I've been singing in my head?! I'm *trying* to focus, Dev, I just—"

Devon raised his voice to match Julian's. "Then *try* harder." He forced himself to calm down but did not lower his tone. "Come on, Jules, you're better than this. I know you are; you know you are. Now you need to stop making excuses and get it together—"

"Excuses?!" Julian shoved a pile of bloody tissues across the table. "You think I've been making excuses? You think these are excuses?"

"You know that's not what I meant. I know you're trying. I'm as frustrated as you. We need to figure this out."

Rae folded her arms on the table and dropped her head down with a miserable *plop*. She'd been positioned in the middle of the two of them like a referee for the last hour. But so far, all they'd managed to do was get each other very, very angry. She'd tried to do what Julian was doing, but her time with his ability was limited. She hadn't developed his tatù nearly as far as he had. She didn't have the skill yet. "Guys, shouting isn't going to help anything! You both need to calm down."

It was like she hadn't even spoken.

"I think those are evidence of a six-hour failure, and we both know you're better than that, Julian! Now, I don't know what else to try with you. I've been patient, I've been supportive—"

Julian's eyebrows shot up. "This is *supportive*? Well, thanks, mate, I never knew you had it in you." He shot Rae a sarcastic look. "What the hell must it be like to date him? I'm sorry, Rae. I didn't realize what you must go through day to day."

She put her fingers to her temples. "Why don't you both take a break for a minute? Walk it off or something."

"Don't make this about Rae," Devon growled. "Just leave her out of it."

"I'm trying to make a point—"

"THAT'S ENOUGH!" Rae shouted. "STOP IT!"

Both boys stared at her in shock as she suddenly pushed to her feet. Across the lounge, a nine-hundred-year-old bartender glanced up from his reading, but she was pretty sure he neither understood nor cared what was going on.

"Don't you get it?" she demanded, finally pushed past her limit. "This isn't about either one of you. One of *these people*," she slammed her hand down on the list of hybrids, "is going to die unless we pull together as a team to stop it. Now, maybe that doesn't mean much to either one of you. Maybe you'd just like to keep fighting here like a couple of idiots, but it means something to me. Maybe because I'm the one who's going to have to live with the outcome *forever*!" She tossed back her dark hair and glared at each one of them in turn, taking grim satisfaction as they cowered like little school boys in the shadow of her rage.

"Julian, please. Keep trying. Do whatever it takes. And Devon," she added quickly as he turned to his friend with a smirk, "leave him alone. You can see he's trying; he's bleeding all over the table for Pete's sake. Give him some space."

Julian returned Devon's smirk with one of his own, and, with a murmured, "Yes, ma'am," they headed their separate ways. When they had both vanished, and Rae stood alone at the table, she turned again to the bartender. He was watching her now with something close to respect.

"Men, you know?"

He blinked, clearly lost on the entire conversation the three of them had just had.

Upstairs, Molly was still asleep. The heavy weight of the list had settled on each of the four friends in turn, stressing them past the brink and forcing them to cope in their own, unique ways. Molly, for example, had developed the sleeping habits of a depressed house cat.

"Hey," Molly mumbled sleepily as Rae slipped inside. "The boys still yelling at each other downstairs?"

"Yep," Rae answered, staring at her reflection in the mirror and pinching her cheeks to get a little color back into them. She looked as pale as a ghost.

"Julian hasn't seen anything yet?"

Rae sighed. "Nope. And, at this rate, I'm not sure if he will. This Cromfield thing is completely undermining his confidence. You know, I'm almost at the point where I think that we should just head to the next place, start warning people as quickly as we can. Not that *I* don't have confidence in Julian, but he's working himself to the bone—more like to the blood—trying to pick this horrible man's brain apart. It isn't healthy, and it's not bloody working. I don't know, maybe on a basic level we should just...? Molls...?" She turned around to see her friend snoring loudly beneath the comforter. Her face fell as she bit her lip and turned back around. "Right."

Taking care to keep quiet, she gathered her purse and tied her long hair back in a ponytail before heading into the hall, locking the door behind her. While it might feel miserable in her weather-inappropriate clothes, the Bolivian climate was doing amazing things for her hair—curling it naturally in a way that she and Molly would take hours to stop back in London. She flicked a stray lock off her forehead and headed to the stairs.

Devon was also on his way down.

"Are you going down there to bother him again?" she accused, pointing a finger at his chest when he stopped and waited for her to catch up.

"No," he said quickly, "I was going to try to find you." A rather roguish grin crept up the side of his face and his eyes twinkled as he stared down at her. "That was quite the speech you gave. I didn't know you had it in you, Rae Kerrigan."

She grinned reluctantly back. "Yeah, you two bloody deserved it! What were you thinking? Howling at each other like a pack of wild dogs."

"I was trying the tough-love approach."

Her delicate eyebrows shot up to her hair and she put her hands on her hips. "The tough-love approach? Really? That's the best you've got?"

He chuckled and clasped his hands together before lowering his circled arms around her waist. "That's the best I've got." He pulled her closer and kissed the top of her head. "I just hate waiting, you know? I'd rather be moving, hitting the action right in the face. I'm better at fighting, saving the day, charging straight into the path of the enemy."

"Well," she smiled coquettishly up at him, "I can help you out with at least one of those..."

He inclined his head with a slow grin, bringing his lips to hers. "Is that right?"

"That's right," she whispered. She waited until he'd closed his eyes before smacking him in the cheek. His eyes flew open and she stared back with a smirk. "I didn't say which one..."

He chuckled again, rubbing his jaw. "Nicely played, Kerrigan."

She moved to the side; she'd barely touched his face and knew it didn't hurt him. She wouldn't have hit him hard, and he knew it as well. She waved over the back of her head as she headed down the stairs. "Leave Julian alone. I'll be back soon."

The Bolivian summer sun temporarily blinded her the second she stepped outside, and she took a moment to adjust. She couldn't get over how different everything was here; from the air, to the temperature, to the people, to the very colors themselves. London was all slate greys and dark blues, even in the summer. But here? She fell in step with the slow-moving crowd heading down the street to the open air market. While the sky was a bright aquamarine, the roads and the houses upon them were a warm shade of rusty brown. Multi-colored blankets and curtains hung from open windows, and every now and then the mismatched diorama would be broken up with a vibrant splash of green.

Rae loved it. She loved the colors, the pace, even the overly-friendly people who waved to her as she passed by their shops. Everything about it was unspoiled; the perfect antithesis of what life was like back in England right now.

But, unfortunately, she and her friends had brought some of that life with them, and she didn't want it to ruin the magic of the city. It was exactly what had brought her to the market. If they were really trying to take every precaution, then step one was simple: they had to blend in.

"Excuse me?" she asked in fluent Spanish as she ducked into a little clothing store. "How much for that jacket? I love it."

The shopkeeper's eyes twinkled as he grabbed it down for her off the rack. "For you, my dear? Half price."

Rae grinned and quickly grabbed three more. Like she'd said, she loved it.

When she got back to the hotel two hours later, decked out with enough clothes for a small army, her friends were nowhere to be seen. The sun was already setting over the hills, dotting the horizon, and she hadn't seen them on the streets. She hastily checked all three rooms, growing more and more anxious with each passing second before she finally went tearing down to the front desk.

"Excuse me," she gasped, reaching full-out panic mode, "do you happen to know where my friends went? There are three of them, two guys and a girl? The girl is tiny; the boys spent the whole day shouting? Both of them are quite handsome. Different kinds of handsome. One is mysterious, long hair, distinct features. The other is dark haired as well, but model-perfect. Fit, tall, gorgeous. He's breath-taking just to look at. I'd have never thought in a million years he'd date someone like me." She blinked suddenly, realizing how ridiculous she sounded.

The old receptionist laughed hoarsely. "Yes, miss, and you didn't have to describe them to me. By now, the entire town knows you're here. The four crazy kids from England."

"Right," Rae mumbled, her face turning red. She'd bought those clothes just in time.

"When I saw them last, they were heading to the pub. Just two doors down."

Rae looked up in surprise. "The pub?" It was the last place she would have guessed.

"Yes, and, at this point, I'd be surprised if you couldn't find them. They're pretty hard to miss. By *looks*, and sound." He chuckled as she thanked him and left.

"Rae! RAE!"

The pub—more of a bar—was a virtual circus, but Rae heard Devon yelling the second she walked inside. Her eyes shot around and found him in an instant, waving as if his life depended on it. All her senses went into overdrive as she darted through the crowded room as quickly as decorum would allow, scanning for signs of trouble along the way. So far, nothing. But Devon's dilated eyes sent chills up her spine.

She pushed herself even faster, rudely elbowing people out of her way. When she finally made it to the other side, she found her boyfriend slumped happily against the wall, holding a half-empty bottle of beer, and sharing a table for two with a man who looked as old as Cromfield should be, had he aged properly.

"Thank goodness you're here!" he gasped before she could say anything. His face was suddenly as serious as she'd ever seen it. "I need to introduce you to Phil."

Phil? Who? What the hell?

"Is this her?" the man named 'Phil' croaked, looking Rae up and down appraisingly.

"Yep," Devon shot him a proud grin, "I told you, right?"

The man nodded slowly, studying Rae's look of surprise with a critical eye. "Well done."

"Cheers!"

They clinked bottles as Rae stared on in amazement.

"What the...?" She grabbed the bottle from Devon's hand just as she realized the table between them was littered with at least twenty more. "Are you...are you *drunk?*"

Phil leaned forward like some sort of coach. "Now, this is where you need to set a precedent," he said wisely. "If you give her an inch now, she'll start hounding you for the rest of your married lives."

Rae's mouth fell open. "*Married* lives?" She turned to Devon, who promptly turned a sickly shade of green. "What exactly have you been telling this guy?!"

"I didn't say we were *married*," he recovered quickly, pulling himself unsteadily to his feet, "I just said I *wanted* us to be married."

Her heart froze in her chest as he stared back at her with an unfocused smile. "You..." she began hesitantly, trying to get a handle on things. "You know what? You know what's really great about what you just said?"

He draped his arm heavily across her shoulders and pulled her in for a sloppy kiss. "What's that, darling?"

She stroked his face sympathetically as he smiled sweetly into her eyes. "You, *darling*, are not going to remember a bit of this in the morning."

He scoffed, as if she was being ridiculous, before turning back to her with a suddenly blank expression, clearly having no idea what they were just talking about. "Sorry...what?"

She fought the urge to roll her eyes, and put a supportive arm around his waist as she guided him drunkenly to a table in the corner. "Don't you worry about it." She glanced back with a sarcastic wave. "Nice meeting you, Phil."

"Prost!" he toasted her.

"Now," she said as she settled Devon into a chair, "what inane part of you thought it would be a good idea to get wasted at the local Bolivian bar?"

The kinds of questions a girl had to ask her boyfriend...

"Come on, Rae," he slurred, twirling her hair clumsily between his fingers, "you basically told me to go."

She pulled back with an incredulous look on her face. "What? How in the world do you figure that?"

"You told me to go find Julian."

"I told you to stay away from Julian!"

He patted her arm consolingly. "I knew what you meant. Anyway, he was so tired and frustrated with this whole 'visions' thing, he decided to come over here to blow off some steam. He asked Molly if she wanted to come, too, and you know I couldn't leave those two alone." He hiccupped adorably. "There's no telling what sort of shenanigans they could get themselves into."

For the first time since she got there, Rae looked around, suddenly remembering that Devon was not the only one to have strayed off the reservation that night.

The hotel receptionist was right. It was almost too easy to find them.

Molly was sitting on a throne-like chair in the middle of the room, preaching a group of rough-and-tumble men a sermon on what sounded suspiciously like shoes. "...And so, it's really just more about finding the right pair of heels for *you*, you know? You find the heels, you find yourself. It's kind of an existench...existall—Julian, what's the word?"

"Existential," he murmured, his eyes never leaving the wall.

Julian was heavily involved in what looked like a game of darts, only most of the darts were broken on the floor, and the thing he was aiming now with such precision was half a pencil.

"Game point," he muttered to the lethal-looking man standing at his side. "If I miss this, you pick me up in the morning and I'll help you fix your roof."

"Um..." Rae jumped up quickly to intervene, taking the pencil from his hand, "I'm sorry, but I think he's going to have to pass on this one. Sorry, boys."

There was a small outcry as she led Julian to the table, and the colossus that had been standing at his side put a heavy hand on her shoulder. "Hey there, lady! We weren't finished. Your friend here owes me a serious debt if he misses this shot."

Rae sighed and picked up a broken dart from the floor. "This shot?" she asked impatiently, gesturing to the target. "From here?"

The man smirked. "That's right. You want to take it for him? See if you can hit the board, little lady."

With a slow smile, Rae turned to look the man right in the eyes. She was still looking when she pierced the final dart right through the bullseye. There was a loud cheering behind her, but she never broke contact with the man's dumbfounded face. "All debts paid. You have a good night now." She smiled sweetly, leaving them in applause behind her.

Now to get Molly... Who knows what the little renegade is up to now?

"The thing is, now there are all these expectations, you know? We're going to be living in the same city, just like ten minutes away, and I don't know how it changes things. I don't even know how it's *supposed* to change things!" Molly threw up her hands with a little sigh, turning with tears to an ancient man sitting beside her. "And Luke is just the sweetest guy. I don't want to mess it up."

The man nodded slowly, keeping his eyes closed so long that Rae thought he might have fallen asleep, before his lips cracked open and he muttered something inaudible in Spanish.

Molly's eyes grew wide as she nodded up and down. "You're so right, Eduardo. I never even thought about it that way. Do you think that we could exchange emails or—"

"Molls?" Rae popped up behind her and clapped her on the arms. "The guys and I got a table over there in the corner. You want to come?"

"In a minute..." The pint-sized girl downed the rest of her whiskey, her enormous eyes still locked on Eduardo like he was pure magic. "I think this is where I'm supposed to make the right decision Eduardo—hey!"

Rae picked her up with a strength that might have seemed strange to any other audience, except everyone in the tiny bar was drunk out of their minds. Carrying Molly across the room so her feet barely touched the peanut-shell-covered floor, she plopped her down beside Julian at the table. "So," she said expectantly, looking at each one of them in turn, "it seems you all decided to go a little crazy tonight. Hmm?" She expected remorse, prepared herself for a long list of excuses from all three of them. What she wasn't expecting were the next words out of Molly's mouth.

"I think I found my spirit guide..."

It was like the exclamation opened the floodgates. The next second, all three of them started talking over each other, so wrapped up in their own stories they hardly noticed.

"I'm done with my visions. I want to start doing work with my hands. Geo and the rest of the guys are roofing some houses on the other side of town tomorrow, and I think I might join."

"You know that Phil's been married eight times? I think that makes him an expert. Or maybe it makes him the worst person in the world to talk to about it. What do you guys think? I wonder if I should go and talk to him again."

"...and then he looked me in the eyes, and I just *knew* he understood what I was saying. It was like he was seeing into my very soul..."

Feeling a bit like the only person in the room not on crazy pills, Rae held up her hand. The others fell silent, watching her in various states of intoxication, waiting to see what she'd do next.

But looking around at their faces, she didn't know herself.

This was too much to ask of them, she understood that. Too much pressure to place on the shoulders of four teenagers. Her eyes flickered between their white knuckles, and the sleep-loss bruises under their eyes. It would be too much for anyone. This was to be expected.

They needed a break? Needed to take a second to breathe? Well, so did she.

"I think I'll have a whiskey."

Three hours later, the four of them were sitting in the hotel lounge. They had been forced to relocate when the bar shut down, but, as the boys quickly discovered, the lounge also served drinks.

Julian grinned as he topped off Molly's drink. "This...this is the good stuff."

Molly downed it in one shot and made a face. "It tastes like death."

"It's supposed to."

Rae laughed and sipped at a drink of her own. "How do you know about all this stuff? I mean, we all went to Guilder together. I'm fairly sure there's not a secret underground cocktail lounge."

"That you know of." Devon winked.

Julian threw back a shot and grimaced. "Actually, I had this for the first time with you, Dev, in where was it...? Uganda? That burned-out stable? The diplomat's daughter?"

Rae turned to Devon with raised eyebrows, but he was quick to change the subject. "So, Molls, you getting dating advice from the locals now? I heard you talking about Luke."

"Yeah, so? Who am I supposed to get advice from?" She gestured to the rest of them with a giggle. "You guys are about as 'star-crossed' as you can get, and you, Julian? Didn't your last date stand you up at graduation?"

Rae giggled at the look on Julian's face, while Devon clapped his shoulder in a way obviously meant to be supportive, but ended up spilling his entire drink.

"Angel," Julian said with a sigh, wiping the table with a napkin.

"Wait," Rae hiccupped, "her name's Angel?"

"Well, Angela, but Angel for short."

Devon grinned. "Wait a minute... *Angel*, Angel? The girl with the—"

Julian flashed him a look. "Yes," he said quickly, "*that* Angel."

Molly was all over it. "The girl with the what?" she demanded. When Julian ignored her, she slammed her glass down, spilling her own drink all over both him and the table. "Julian, seer of all things, you tell me!"

He laughed and picked up the napkin again, thoroughly drenched in whiskey. "Angel's inked like the rest of us. She has a tatù."

"A really awesome one," Devon prompted with a grin.

Julian rolled his eyes. "She could stun people. Freeze them in place with only a touch. Kind of like our PC Tasers."

Rae giggled. "And is that how she got you, Jules? Did she stun you to the core?"

"No..." his cheeks flushed with a sudden, incriminating grin. "She saved that for later."

"What?!" Molly shrieked, clapping her hands together.

"So what happened?" Rae asked curiously. She couldn't imagine any girl in their right mind breaking up with Julian.

"I don't know," he said, looking suddenly thoughtful, "I didn't see her decide to do it. But I try not to sneak into people's heads when I have a choice."

His face suddenly clouded, and Rae's heart went out to him.

Yeah...except lately.

As usual, Devon seemed to be mirroring her thoughts. "Maybe we should all try to get some sleep," he suggested. "Start fresh again in the morning."

Rae nodded, pushing gingerly to her feet. "That's a good idea."

"I'll say..." Molly yawned widely and lay her head down on the sticky table. "Goodnight."

Julian chuckled softly and picked her up. "I think you'd regret that come morning. 'Night, guys," he called as he carried her up the stairs.

Finally alone, Devon leaned in and gave Rae a quick kiss before they headed up the stairs themselves, walking hand in hand. Despite their close proximity with this shared mission, Rae felt like she hadn't had a second alone with him in a thousand years.

Maybe that's because whenever you're together, you get all weird about the future.

She pushed her annoying subconscious to the furthest reaches of her brain and settled down beside Devon on the bed. It surprised her how quickly she had fallen into this 'coupley' routine. Get finished with a long day's work, head home, curl up with her boyfriend in bed.

On most days, she couldn't think of anything better.

After getting the news of her immortality, she had to admit it had become a bit strained.

It wasn't tonight, though. The liquor had done its trick, and the two of them stretched out on the rickety mattress without a care in the world, coming together in a tangle of limbs and kisses. His breath was sweet with whiskey, and she smiled to herself at some of the more outrageous things he'd done tonight. First there was his impromptu 'drink-off' with Julian the second they'd gotten back to the lounge, then there was when she'd heard him gravely explaining his 'super powers' to a dog lingering outside the bar, and then, well, then there was when she'd first walked in and he'd told some guy named Phil that he wanted to marry her.

The smile froze on her face as she tried to sort out how she felt about this. Of course, he was drunk, that had to be taken into account. But it wasn't like alcohol put ideas like that into your head. It tended to unlock them and get people talking about them freely. Either way, there was a very good chance that he wouldn't remember a thing about it the next day.

But she would. In fact, she didn't think she could ever forget.

Marriage. Devon had said he wanted to *marry* her.

At this point, what did that even mean?

"What're you thinking about?" he murmured, bringing her wrist up to his lips and kissing it.

She smiled. "You. And me. Us."

"*Us*, huh?" He grinned. "Anything in particular?"

"You know; the works." She stared at him steadily for a moment before looking quickly away. Nope, she couldn't do this now. It was one huge emotional milestone too many. "So I got us some clothes in town today. I shopped when you three were devoting yourselves to a new life of South American alcoholism."

He laughed. "If my short-term memory can recall, you got on that train pretty quick yourself."

"It's not the same thing," she scoffed teasingly. "My liver is constantly healing and regenerating itself. I'm not doing any long-term damage. Besides, it's not like it can—"

...kill me.

She froze in place, unable to say another word. Her very blood seemed to cool in her veins, and, despite the fact that she was lying next to Devon in bed, she suddenly felt very much alone.

The next second, Devon's hand came up and cupped her cheek. "Rae, we're going to figure this out. I swear it. We just need to figure out where Cromfield—"

There was a sudden banging on their door, and they pulled apart. Unable to withstand the pressure, the flimsy wood sprang open, leaving Julian silhouetted in its wake.

He stared at them, his eyes bright. "I know where Cromfield's going next!"

Chapter 5

They left sometime in the middle of the night. Way before the sun came up. Before the old receptionist even had a chance to wonder whatever became of those four crazy English kids. The clothes Rae had bought for sticking around in South America got tossed in the trash as they climbed aboard a flight to Budapest— Molly still cursing the 'gods of whiskey' and occasionally vomiting in the airplane bathroom.

If Julian had been having trouble seeing the future before, he'd more than made up for it now. There was an intensity about him that Rae had never seen, an assertive force that had him pushing them all forward. The second they got out in public, the sunglasses went back on as he started examining Cromfield's every minute decision and how it would lead them to the next person on the list.

They developed a kind of strategy, where Rae and Devon would take Julian by the arms, leading him as though he was blind, because he was in a trance so often now. It worried Rae, but she was scared to voice her concerns. She'd tried to use Julian's tatù while the others were resting, with no success. She was months behind his ability, if not years. He'd used his daily since he'd turned sixteen. She tried his, maybe, a handful of times over the past few years. It didn't matter at the moment; he was using it to find Cromfield, and they had to find a way to keep moving, regardless.

After Budapest came Sydney, after Sydney they travelled to Spain. In each country, it seemed as though they arrived just in the nick of time. Julian would see that Cromfield was on his way, but they would always find the hybrids first. The small step ahead of Cromfield gave them enough time to warn the hybrids of the danger and convince them to go into hiding.

Luckily enough, none of the hybrids or their parents seemed to question the danger for even an instant. Most had been pre-conditioned by the laws of the tatù world, that when Rae told them there was trouble on the way they didn't hesitate before packing their bags. She wondered if there were schools like Guilder in each country, or if undercover agencies like the Privy Council existed elsewhere. She never got the chance to ask. These weren't social gatherings, and they didn't have time to dig for information. She just hoped word wouldn't get back to the Privy Council and they would come hopping back after them. She wanted to stop Cromfield and find Jennifer and change the world. It just couldn't be done in a day.

She hated knocking on people's doors to tell them they were in grave danger. She often watched them go with a mixed feeling of relief and a strange kind of detached sadness.

Was this what her life would have been? If her mother hadn't been brainwashed, would they have eventually had to move somewhere different to keep their secret? Or keep moving around place to place. Just to keep *her* secret? Would they have assumed different names, different identities? One day, the same as any other, would people like Rae and Devon have come knocking to tell her to run? Would her father have hunted her down?

Another thought nearly knocked the breath out of her. Had Cromfield done the same to her father? Had he changed Simon Kerrigan into the monster he became? What if he had been just like her, cursed with a hybrid tatù, only to have it tainted by the evil? What had happened to him?

Julian had them rushing off to the next country before she even had a chance to voice her thoughts; not that she would have said them out loud. Everyone believed her father to be a terrible monster, almost as bad as Cromfield. She was beginning to question it, and hoped she'd have the chance to talk to her mother once they stopped Cromfield. If he was even stoppable. Once they caught up to him, what would they do? The guy could live forever. Killing him wasn't an option.

She focused on the task at hand, happy for the distraction from her own inner turmoil. The more countries they visited, the more names they checked off their list. Only one thing remained a constant: Rae Kerrigan was never meant to have a normal life.

"Come on, Julian, just take it easy," Rae murmured to her buddy. She and Devon were discreetly propping him up in an airport food court, after he had suddenly slipped into a trance standing in line to get a slice of pizza.

Molly had run off to get coffee, so Rae used Maria's telepathy to send her a mental message to bring a stack of napkins.

Rae stared at Julian's comatose body. It looked like this vision was even more intense than the usual.

"I can't watch him do this anymore." Devon ground his teeth together as he lowered his friend gently into a chair. Julian's head slumped forward, and Devon's face tightened in pain. "It's hurting him! I think this is gonna kill him eventually." His voice broke with emotion and tiredness.

"I know," Rae said quietly. "I don't want him doing it anymore either." She stroked back a lock of Julian's long dark hair, tucking it into his ponytail. "But you heard what he said: now that his tatù's working again, he's staying the course. He wants to see this through."

Devon sighed. "Of course he *wants* to. I just don't know if we should let him."

Rae laughed. She couldn't help it. "Do you realize how stubborn he is? How stubborn you are?"

Devon raised a single eyebrow. "Isn't that the pot calling the kettle?"

"I'm not stubborn!" She grinned when she realized how she sounded. She glanced at Julian. "What're we going to do with him?" Rae teased lightly, happy to have a moment of comic relief. "Medically-induced coma? How do you stop something that's going on inside his head?"

At that moment the future "released" him, and Julian came back to the present with a gasp. A curious family paused from walking, and watched with concern as Julian slumped forward onto the table, bleeding profusely from the nose.

Devon waved them away, and, fortunately, Molly came back at that very moment with the napkins.

"Aw, sweetie," she murmured, mopping up his face, "you're always such a mess now. And to think, I used to think you were so handsome..."

Julian laughed weakly at her teasing, not realizing that beneath the joke lay real concern. The same concern was mirrored in Devon and Rae's eyes.

The laughter of a moment ago disappeared. Rae's chest felt heavy with worry. He was overdoing it. This was becoming too dangerous. You could only delve into someone else's future so far before there was no coming back to your own time. She opened her mouth, ready to suggest they contact the Privy Council, and then closed it. What if *they* pushed him harder than he was already pushing himself?

"Sorry to disappoint you," he panted, gratefully taking the coffee Molly pressed into his hands and gulping down the top inch. If it was burning hot, he didn't notice.

"Hey, future boy," Devon said quietly. "Did you see where we're supposed to go next?"

After racing back to the airport from a mission in Mali, Julian's visions had suddenly cut short, and they were stuck in a holding pattern. According to him, it was as if the trail just suddenly went blank. As if Cromfield was no longer living, or at least, no longer thinking. They had been sitting at the airport for the last day and a half, which was why this sudden vision in the food court had caught everyone so off-guard.

"Yeah, he's heading to—" Suddenly, Julian's voice cut off and he gripped his head in pain. His eyes screwed up, and he opened his mouth in a silent cry before biting his lip very hard to keep from making a sound.

"Jules!" Rea knelt in front of his chair in alarm. "What's happening? What can I do?"

"My head," he gasped. "It's like someone's ripping open my head!"

Devon looked around, pale with fright. "That's it. I'm taking you to a hospital."

Rae grabbed his hand as Julian doubled over onto the table, moaning. "What good would that do? A non-tatù doctor will have no idea what to do with him."

"But his pain is real—"

"Exactly," Molly interrupted. "And at a hospital, they would prescribe morphine." She looked at Rae expectantly, and, after a moment of confused silence, she cocked her head towards Julian. "Give him morphine, Rae. Use Ethan's ink."

Of course! Good old Dollar Bill... Focusing very hard on the freshman's ability, Rae held her hand beneath the table and conjured a syringe. Inside, a clear liquid bubbled into existence before cooling at the speed of light.

It was here that she paused, looking at Julian uncertainly. "I've...I've never given anyone a shot before. I don't know—"

"I'll do it." Devon took the syringe, and, in one fluid movement, plunged it deep into his friend's leg. Julian visibly relaxed as the drug entered his system, and a second later he was calm.

"How're you doing, buddy?" Rae asked breathlessly, watching his every move, terrified she'd made too much in the syringe. They had no idea what they were doing. What if she killed him with an O.D.? *Sheesh! Rash and idiotic.* That's what she was turning into. "How's your head? You okay?"

"Rae?" He stared at her for a moment, slightly unfocused, before his face brightened with a huge smile. "Rae." His lips formed a perfect "O" as he repeated her name. "Rae's a beautiful name!"

She and Devon exchanged a quick look before turning to Molly, who raised her hands innocently and avoided their gaze. "And...it can also make you a little loopy."

"A *little* loopy?" Devon hissed as Julian started absent-mindedly stroking his jacket.

"What were we supposed to do?" Molly countered. "Did you want him to be in pain? They gave that stuff to my Aunt Pam after her knee surgery, and it worked great."

Rae frowned in concern as Julian began licking the outside of his coffee cup. "How great?"

"Well, she did claim to see flying cats for the next few hours—"

"Molly?!" Rae cried as Devon hissed, "A *few* hours?"

"We need to go to Texas."

Wait... what?

Everyone turned to Julian at once as he made this declaration. After a moment, he realized all eyes were on him, and he looked behind himself in concern. "Is somebody coming?" he whispered loudly. "Should we run?"

"No, no, everything's fine," Devon assured him, fighting back the urge to laugh. Rae was resisting the same urge. "Why should we go to Texas, Jules? Is that where Cromfield is going?"

"They have great barbeque."

Devon flashed Rae a pained look. "Kerrigan?"

"I've got this." With a calming smile, she took Julian's hands in her own. "Hey, Jules, I want you to think about Texas, okay? Can you think about it for me?" She slipped into Carter's gift, and a moment later, she was barreling down the complex corridors of Julian's mind. She raced past flashes of people and places: Guilder and the graduation, her and their other friends, a beautiful white-haired girl who was leaning in to kiss him. Then on, faster and faster. Her hands tightened around his, and she found herself bracing slightly against the sudden change in tone. There was a pull, a mental pressure pushing her down. She fought to get above it, and when she saw an image of what looked to be the old American South, she latched on.

There was Cromfield, alright. Getting off a plane in Dallas and glancing down at a scribbled address written on the side of the map. As Rae—through Julian's eyes—leaned forward to get a better look, Cromfield looked up suddenly and stared straight at her.

At least, stared straight *past* her. Because he couldn't be actually *seeing* Julian, could he? He couldn't know that Julian was watching. Devon said that was impossible...

A pair of strong hands ripped hers away from Julian's, and she opened her eyes to see Devon pulling her away in concern. Julian opened his eyes at the same time, still loopy from the drugs, but before he slipped away into narcotics bliss, she could have sworn she saw a glimmer of fear.

"Sweetie, you're bleeding."

She glanced up at Devon before reaching for her nose. Sure enough, blood. "It's nothing," she said quickly, not quite understanding what had just happened, but knowing, deep down, it wasn't good.

"Here." Molly handed her a napkin and watched as she dabbed at her face. "So Cromfield's in Texas? Is that what Julian saw?"

"Yeah," Rae panted, still trying to catch her breath. "He's going to Texas."

As for the other part, she wasn't sure what exactly Julian saw...

"Why do they call it the Lone Star State?" Molly asked curiously as they pulled away from the airport rent-a-car in style.

The only car available on such short notice had been a black-tinted Escalade which Devon had rented without a thought. A little flashy, perhaps, but Rae had to admit, under the blinding Texan sun, the windows were a welcome relief.

"Because no one wants to live here," Julian muttered, slapping on the air conditioning. The morphine had worn off somewhere over the Atlantic, and to say he was grumpy would be understating it by a couple thousand miles.

He hadn't talked to Rae about what had happened, what she had seen. To be honest, she wasn't sure if he even remembered it happening, but somehow, she thought he did. There was something a little too deliberate in the way he was avoiding her eyes.

"So it's Wichita Falls, Texas?" Devan asked, programming it into the navigator.

Julian nodded. "Yep. A little rodeo town." He flashed his first, albeit rather sarcastic, smile since landing. "Should be fun."

"It *will* be fun." Molly nudged him, determined to lighten the mood. "I might have to buy us some hats. Like cowboy hats, and boots. Leather chaps for Devon. Oh! I couldn't get wranglers. I heard they're very fashionable in Texas." She babbled on and then started complaining when her phone died and she couldn't search the Internet anymore.

About two hours later, they rolled into town. The sun had just started to set over the trees, and Rae was about to ask where they should start looking first, when she realized that almost every car in the tiny city was parked in front of what looked to be the most 'happening' bar in Texas.

"What do you think?" Molly asked as the car rolled to a stop. Julian rolled down his window and the four friends peered out at the noisy club. "Should we give it a try?"

"Couldn't hurt." Devon parked and got out of the car.

"It's better than searching the barns," Julian agreed and stretched. "Plus I could use a drink. Or two."

Molly and Rae giggled at his caustic teasing, but Rae hung back a step and caught his arm as the four of them headed inside. They needed to talk, even if it was just for a second, even if it was the last thing either of them wanted. She had to know what the hell was going on.

"What's up?" He looked down at her in surprise.

She hesitated, a little thrown off her game by his open nonchalance. He'd been high as a kite on morphine when she'd gone inside his mind. Maybe he really didn't remember.

Then his arm stiffened nervously and her eyes narrowed in triumph.

Oh, hell yes, he did remember! "Listen, Jules, we need to talk—"

"Guys! You coming?" Devon called from the door.

Julian tugged his arm away and headed swiftly up the steps. "Yup."

Rae stood behind, seething in the darkness. *Oh, that little—*

"Rae?" Devon cocked his head curiously.

"Yeah! I'm coming!"

Despite the huge crowd roaring in the bar, which on the inside looked like an abandoned sort of factory, it was surprisingly easy to hear. This wasn't just because Rae was using Devon's fennec fox tatù; it was because the place was separated into clearly delineated sections. There was the restaurant area, the bar area, the pool and darts area, and what sounded like some sort of gladiatorial rink at the end. Rae avoided this one with a shudder and turned to her friends.

"Okay. So we know her name is Camille Lachaise, she's about nineteen years old, and her tatù is...well, unknown. Let's spread out, okay? Look for anyone who could match the description."

Devon cleared his throat, looking abruptly uncomfortable. "Yeah...uh...there's no need."

"Why?"

He nodded over her shoulder, and Rae looked around towards the gladiatorial pit she'd been avoiding thus far. It wasn't some sort of death arena, as her warped imagination had previously thought, but there was a crowd of people cheering someone on in the center of a ring. Confused, she edged closer, weaving her way through the mob until she was at the very front.

Her jaw dropped wide open.

She had never seen anyone ride a mechanical bull before.

Chapter 6

For a full minute, the Rae stared in open astonishment at the spectacle before her. Devon, Julian, and Molly crowded around behind her, probably doing the same thing.

It was easy to see why Devon had quickly identified the girl as Camille. Every time the bull shot its metal legs up into the air, she lurched forward, revealing a giant tatù on her lower back. Rae shook her head; in her opinion Camille was showing way more than just her ink. Of course, everyone cheering in the crowded bar thought it was an actual tattoo, but the Guilder students knew better.

Slipping into another tatù of her own—Madame Elpis' hawk eyes—Rae leaned forward to get a better glimpse. It was a very interesting ink, that much was sure, but she couldn't really figure out what it stood for. It looked to be something like a fist; a streamlined arm of pure muscle slamming down on the top of her low-riding jeans. However, the strange part was the depiction of the air around the fist. It was like one of those children's books full of holograms, where, if you tilted the page, you saw a slightly different version of the same design. That and the almost invisible waving lines emanating from the powerful design made it look like her entire lower back was shimmering.

Tatùs weren't usually that big. Except Rae's. She had one maybe slightly bigger than Camille's.

There was a collective gasp from the crowd as the mechanical bull suddenly stood up on its front feet, bucking its back to the sky. This was obviously the point in the show where even the most skilled riders would be sent flying.

Nonetheless, the girl stayed harnessed.

She held on as easily as if it was standing still, waving her arm enthusiastically to the crowd and shrieking with drunken laughter. Money changed hands as bets were paid while the bull slowly wound down to a stop. She hopped off and flipped back her bouncy brown curls, taking a wad of twenties from a burly-looking man before making her way, grinning, to the bar.

"Well, go on, Julian." Molly gave him a nudge. "Go charm her."

"Me?" He hesitated, looking a little daunted. "Why does it have to be me?"

An image of the white-haired Angela flashed through Rae's mind and she gave him an accusatory smirk. "Oh, that's right, Julian likes blondes."

He shot her a nervous glare, and opened his mouth like he was about to say something, when Devon sighed and stepped forward. "I'll see what I can do."

This time it was Julian who smirked as Rae stepped back, her arms folded tightly across her chest. Obviously, using her boyfriend as bait to lure a sexy rodeo star wasn't exactly what she'd had in mind.

Devon slid onto the bar stool beside Camille, cutting in front of a long line of other men, and smiled politely at the side of her head. Rae switched tatùs to hear their conversation better. "That was a hell of a show," Devon said as he grinned at the girl, showing his dimple. "Mind if I buy you a drink?"

Camille's shoulders tensed as she sighed. "Listen, buddy, just 'cause I rode the bull doesn't mean I'm just up for—" She stopped dead when she turned and saw him for the first time. "Well aren't you just the cutest thing I ever did see!" Her eyes grew wide and she tapped the tip of his nose with a red-manicured fingernail. She shot him a huge smile. "Of course I'll get a drink with you. Truth be told, sugar, I'd be down for just about anything you'd like to do tonight. You ever grab the bull by the horns?"

Rae's fingers curled into automatic fists. "Well...isn't that sweet," she growled under her breath.

Across the bar, Devon flinched apologetically—he could hear her just as well as she could hear him. He shifted slightly and winked at Camille. "Why don't we just start out with a drink?" he said easily, grabbing two whiskeys from across the bar and leaving his money on the counter.

Camille slid her arm seductively into his as he led her across the room and to the booth on the far side of the building. She stopped short when she saw Julian, Rae, and Molly all sitting there, smiling politely. Except for maybe Rae, whose smile was clearly forced.

"Friends of yours?" she asked cautiously. She took a step back, and, much to Rae's surprise, and annoyance, Devon fell back with Camille, his arm still intertwined with hers.

"Uh, yeah," he recovered quickly, eyes flickering down to her arm with a slight frown. "We're road-tripping to California, just passing through. This is Julian, Molly, and Rae."

If Camille noticed the tender way he said Rae's name, she certainly didn't let on. Instead, she sat down at an empty seat, pulling him possessively with her.

"Well, that sounds like a lot of fun," she said brightly. "And why exactly are you heading to California, when you could stay in Texas?" She winked at Devon.

He stiffened slightly, but maintained a fixed smile as she lifted her hand up and started playing with the back of his hair. "Actually, I guess you could say we're on a little mission," he said charmingly. "We're going from town to town, looking for people... like us."

Her hand froze behind him, but she maintained a careful smile. "People like *you*? And what would that be, sugar? Hot little Gypsies with sexy accents?"

"Gypsies," Molly said purposely, leaning toward Camille, but still keeping a safe distance. She scoffed. "*I* do not dress like a travelling-dancing person or whatever Gypsies do. We travel on a different mission. We're look for people with interesting...*tattoos*."

In the blink of an eye, Camille slammed Devon's head *through* the varnished tabletop.

"HEY!" Rae screamed, leaping to her feet as the girl rushed through the door. In the general chaos of the bar, no one else even noticed.

Julian's eyes glassed over for a fraction of a second, before he muttered, "Red truck, white streaks." Then he knelt quickly on the floor to attend to Devon.

In a rage, Rae rushed out into the night, Molly fast on her heels. She could just barely make out the girl's bouncing curls as she ducked into the driver's seat of a red truck with white racing stripes drawn on the side. Without stopping to think, Rae fired a bolt of lightning at the tires. It wouldn't have made such a devastating impact, except that Molly had done the exact same thing. Pieces of rubber shot into the air as the two back tires exploded, dropping the bed of the truck onto the pavement with a pitiful shriek. In a cloud of sparks, the whole thing rocked to a sudden stop.

Molly took a nervous step backwards, half-angling herself behind Rae as the silhouette of the girl slowly climbed out of the truck. Rae was incensed, the image of her boyfriend's bloodied face flashing through her mind.

Camille took one look at the singed wheels before storming back towards the bar. The air around her seemed to shimmer the closer she got, and it wasn't long before Rae felt a strange tingling sensation prickling along her skin. This girl had some a seriously good tatù. Maybe as good as hers, but not quite. And hell, she was going to take it!

"Aw, darling," Camille drawled dangerously, "you have no idea who you just picked a fight with."

Rae pulled herself up to her full height, her eyes flashing in the night. "Neither do you, cowgirl."

"Yeah, except we don't want to fight—remember, Rae?" Molly whispered from behind her.

Rae cocked her head to the side as Camille cracked her knuckles. "One problem, Molls: this girl likes to put on a show, don't you, Camille?"

Camille froze in her tracks before taking another threatening step forward. "How do you know my name?"

"Devon told you," Rae said again, regaining a little of her composure and a little less anger. "We came here looking for people like you. You might be in trouble and we're here to help—"

"Devon? Was that his name?" the girl said with a careless grin. "Pretty guy. Probably not so pretty now with his head bashed in—"

With a piercing scream, Rae launched herself at the girl.

Only to immediately fly backwards.

It was like the air itself threw her, vibrating at such a pace that she was lifted off her feet. She landed in a surprised heap fifty feet away, wincing as she instantly pulled herself up again.

Molly's eyes grew wide when Rae had gone flying. She sent a few thousand volts the girl's way before wisely ducking behind a parked car.

"I get it..." Camille laughed as she mocked Rae. "So he's your boyfriend, right?" She laughed harder. "I should've known he was taken—it seemed too good to be true. Y'all picked the wrong girl t' mess with." She sent another shockwave through the pavement, and the car Molly was ducking behind rocked towards her.

Molly stifled a scream and turned to Rae. "Do something!"

Rae shrugged. *The little dirt-bag wants to play that game? Fine!* So Rae disappeared.

Camille's mouth dropped as she whipped her head back and forth, trying to find her. A moment later, it was the flirty cowgirl who went flying through the air. Whatever tatù she had, it clearly wasn't defensive. She had absolutely no protection as she sailed backwards and landed with a muffled crack on the asphalt.

Rae reappeared a few steps in front of her, watching as the girl whimpered and grabbed at her leg. "Listen," Rae panted, "I don't want to hurt you. We only want to talk." She offered Camille a hand, but, instead of taking it, Camille pulled her down with such force that her knees made little craters in the parking lot.

"*Ow!*" Rae shouted, falling back on the ground beside Camille, who clearly couldn't get up.

"Ahh, y'all are a bunch of amateurs."

"Really?" Rae hissed.

Camille watched in amazement as Rae switched into Charles' tatù to heal herself. The blood disappeared as the cuts closed up and vanished before her eyes. With a frustrated sigh, Rae pushed her hair out of her eyes and turned to Camille, ready for round two. But Camille was staring at her as if seeing her for the first time.

"Invisibility, strength, *and* healing?" Her brown eyes locked on Rae's face in sheer astonishment. "What are you?"

"Rae Kerrigan," Rae extended her hand. "Nice to meet you." She figured the Kerrigan name didn't carry strong outside of England.

The girl hesitated for a moment before taking it—a sign of trust. "I'm sorry," she gasped, still gripping her calf. "I didn't mean to hurt you or your friends. It's just...Look, I'm always on the protective side." Her head cocked to the side. She pointed to her back. "You got one of these, too, obviously."

Rae nodded.

Molly cleared her throat, still hiding behind the car, but obviously annoyed. "And so do I."

Camille shook her head, her voice dropping to a whisper, "I've never met anyone like me before. What're you doing here? What do you want with me?"

"Is it safe to come out now?" Molly called out.

Rae chuckled, and even Camille had to grin. Luckily the park lot was still empty. The patrons of the bar preferred the entertainment inside, not out.

Rae turned slightly. "Yeah, Molls, it's cool." But she glanced at Camille warily as Molly made her way towards them. "Hurt her, and I'll end you," she warned under her breath.

Camille held up her hands. "Y'all are good." She smiled wryly. "Besides, this is one fight even I don't think I could win..."

"Molly? Rae?" Julian raced outside, tugging a half-conscious Devon under his arm.

"We're over here!" Rae waved as the boys hurried over.

His dark eyes flickered over Rae's casually reclined position, Camille's injured leg, and Molly's static-ridden hair. "What'd I miss?"

"Just the introduction," Rae answered, helping him lower Devon carefully to the ground.

Devon was having trouble keeping his eyes open, and a steady stream of blood poured down from a cut on his head. "We all good?" he mumbled.

"Devon?" Rae asked anxiously, holding his face up by his chin. "Are you okay? How many fingers am I holding up?"

"Fingers?" His face scrunched up with a dazed smile. "You look hot, Rae. Like, crazy-hot."

Molly and Camille snorted, and even Julian had a hard time keeping it together. Rae shook her head with a worried grin. "He'd better be okay." The unsaid warning had Camille reacting immediately.

"We can go to my house," Camille offered tentatively. "My mom's an emergency room nurse. It's come in handy with all the...well...my power's a little hard to control sometimes."

"Good!" Julian said gratefully. "We'll follow you. Devon's in no condition to drive."

"Actually," Camille's eyes flicked to her truck, "I think my little baby's out of commission for a while. Mind if I ride with you?"

Just like most of the other hybrids they'd come across, Camille's house was perched on the outskirts of town, making it easy to leave at a moment's notice. When Camille limped up the front steps and rang the doorbell, her mother didn't seem surprised. What did surprise her was the slightly bedraggled-looking group huddled along either side.

"Peter," she called without a second's thought, "we've got company."

A tall man stepped into view and opened the door wider, soaking in all the details before he asked, "Cam, are you starting a grunge band or something?"

"Nah, Dad. But they're all good."

With nervous titters of laughter, the five of them made their way inside. Camille marched straight to the medicine cabinet, pulling out a container with a red cross stamped across the front and handing it wordlessly to her mother.

Shaking her head with a little smile, Mrs. Lachaise sat her daughter down at the kitchen table and started examining her leg. "Let me guess—you got thrown off that idiotic bull down at the bar?"

Camille grinned, flinching slightly as her mother wrapped an ace bandage snugly around her knee. "Aw, Mom, you know I never fall."

Mrs. Lachaise looked up sharply. "Well maybe you should start." She gave her daughter a piercing stare before turning her attention to the rest of them. "So does anybody want to tell me what's going on? Or should I just make the rounds and start giving stitches?"

Devon shuddered and half-stepped behind Julian, while Rae pushed past him to stand in front, ready to protect her friends in case Camille's parents reacted the same way Camille had initially. "Mrs. Lachaise, my friends and I are from England."

"I figured," Mrs. Lachaise snapped. "Y'all don't sound Southern."

Rae swallowed. "We came to Texas to talk to you. You see..." she paused, a little uncertain how to go on. By now, her script was mostly memorized, but at least one, if not both, of these parents was gifted with super-strength, and she didn't want to say something that might set them off. "We're like you."

One by one, Devon and Julian rolled up their sleeves, and Molly twisted around to show what lay near the bottom of her shirt. Rae held back, not sure if she should do the same.

An identical look of extreme worry shadowed Camille's parents' faces as they locked onto each design.

Screw it! "Me, too..." Rae turned around and lifted up her own shirt. "Except, I'm more like your daughter."

Camille gasped. "What the heck?"

"We're here to help," Julian assured the parents, and, for the first time, they looked slightly less worried. They sat down and motioned for everyone to do the same.

Camille limped forward eagerly to examine the design on Rae's ink. "Oh, that's beautiful," she murmured, looking at the glittering fairy. "That's way cooler than mine." She turned around to give the four friends a better look of the fist tatù.

"What is it?" Molly asked with a frown. "What can you do?"

"My dad's got super-strength," Camille replied, glancing at her father who nodded once, "while my mom can control vibrations. Put them together, and it can be a kind of lethal combination."

Mrs. Lachaise laughed. "Hence the first aid kit."

"Vibrations?" Devon frowned, shaking his head. "I don't get it."

Camille headed to the kitchen with a smirk. "Watch and learn, handsome." She picked up a plate and laid her hand smoothly over the top. The porcelain began to quake and shiver, and the next moment, it shattered in her hand.

Mrs. Lachaise groaned softly. "I keep telling her not to practice on the plates. I'm going to have to get new ones before long—*again*."

Camille just grinned. "Now imagine doing that...but to a person. Or a car, or a wall. It all ends up the same way. One tatù enhances the other."

Molly and Rae clapped approvingly, seriously impressed, but the boys shared a worried glance that was not lost on either Camille or her parents.

"I know," Camille said as she pre-empted them, her voice suddenly hard, "I'm a Class Five, right?"

"A Class Five?" Rae asked curiously, turning to Devon. "What's that?"

He and Julian shared another look before he said, "The Privy Council has a class system to identify tatùs based on their...destructive capacities. Most people fall somewhere between one and two. Think of Alecia—a diagnostician at the hospital, or Maria with her telepathy; their tatùs are either neutral or can only be used defensively. Then there's Class Threes. That would be like...Haley creating gusts of wind, and Rob turning into an eagle. In fact, unless the animal's particularly dangerous, most shifters fall into Class Three. I'm a Class Three." Devon grinned bashfully. He was perfect in everything, but, here, for what seemed like the first time, he didn't have the highest score.

"What about me?" Molly asked excitedly, eager to find out where she stood.

Devon grinned. "Actually, Molls, you're a Class Four. Your tatù can only be used offensively."

"I knew it! I've been offending people with my tatù since I got it!" she said proudly. Then her face fell as she re-registered the number. "Wait...only a Class Four? Not a—"

"Trust me, you don't want to be a—" Devon stopped suddenly and glanced with a rather guilty expression at Camille, and then Rae. "Sorry...no offense."

Camille held up her hands and laughed. "Some of us gotta shake what our mommas gave us. Literally, in my case."

Rae was still confused. She couldn't believe she hadn't heard of these categories before. "I don't get it though, Dev; why wouldn't you want to be a Class Five?"

This time, it was Mrs. Lachaise who answered. "Class Fives are considered too dangerous to be out and about in society. When they're just young to their ability, they're closely monitored, and, more often than not, by the time they reach adulthood, they've mysteriously 'disappeared' into the black hole of the tatù system. At least in America anyways."

Disappeared?! Did that mean—

"They're not murdered," Devon said quickly, reading Rae's horrified expression. "They're just..." he shifted uncomfortably, "put into holding."

"Holding?" Rae repeated, dumbfounded. "You mean, like, *jail?*"

Again, he fidgeted uneasily, looking at his shoes. "Of sorts..."

"It's what they would've done to Camille," Mr. Lachaise said suddenly. "My little girl would have grown up in some cell. Been experimented on like a lab rat. Matilde and I would have been disciplined just for having her." He whirled around on the four of them in abrupt anger. "That's what your precious Privy Council does. Its long arm reaches across the ocean and snaps the innocent up." He glared at them. "And yes—don't think for a minute I don't recognize the soldiers, the training." His eyes swept them up and down before resting on his daughter with a helpless sort of rage. "It tears apart families. It ruins lives."

Mrs. Lachaise walked over silently and slipped her hand onto his shoulder. "That's why we had to run." She glanced around the tiny two-bedroom house sadly. "Texas isn't ideal...but we wanted to find a place where Camille could still ride horses like she used to do in Rennes."

"Rennes?" Julian asked in surprise. "You lived in France?"

"We left on my sixteenth birthday," Camille replied. "The day I got my ink."

Everyone was quiet for a while until Molly said tentatively, "Well, have you ever considered going to the Privy Council and trying to explain—"

Mrs. Lachaise held up her hand, and Molly fell silent. "We did nothing wrong. You can't help who you fall in love with. The Privy Council has no jurisdiction over the heart. I'm not apologizing for my marriage. Or my family."

Rae couldn't agree more.

"We're not here on behalf of the Privy Council," she said slowly, weighing her words with great care. "To be honest, if they knew where we were, I'm sure they'd drag us back to London in chains. We're here for a different reason entirely. A different kind of danger now lurks. One that has to do with your daughter..."

By now, telling the Cromfield story only took a brief amount of time. The four friends had perfected it; keeping it clear and concise, one person handling the narration before another seamlessly stepped in to take the reins. It was a testament to how much the Lachaises feared the Privy Council, that they would rather take their chances on their own than go to them for help. In fact, every hybrid family Rae and her friends had come across had felt the exact same way. And after hearing the Lachaises' story, Rae couldn't blame them.

"Hey."

She turned around to see Devon walking slowly towards her through the trees. After dinner, she'd gone out for a walk in the orchard behind Camille's house. Julian and Molly were inside helping the Lachaises start to pack, while Mrs. Lachaise had been patching up Devon's head.

"You survived," Rae said with a small smile.

He brought his hand up to his bandaged forehead with a grimace. "Just barely. Remind me *not* to volunteer to buy our mark drinks again. We'll send Julian."

Rae chuckled. "That's what you get for hitting on a cowgirl."

"Aw," his arms circled around her and she leaned back into him, "was somebody jealous?"

"No." Rae sniffed. "But somebody did feel a lot better when she threw said cowgirl thirty feet into the air."

Devon laughed and spun her around for a kiss. "What am I going to do with you?"

She leaned in again, kissing him more slowly this time, savoring every second, but then pulling away suddenly. Her eyes flicked up to his and she asked almost nervously, "Devon...what class am I?"

"You?" The corner of his mouth turned up in a quirky grin. "You'd be, like, a Class Ten. I don't think they have a class for you."

She sighed and turned back out to the trees. "That's what I thought."

"Hey," he squeezed her hand, "nobody's coming for you. Nobody's after you. You're working for the good guys, remember?"

"The good guys..." Her eyes grew hard. "*Right*."

She felt him stiffen behind her. "What's that supposed to mean?"

"Dev," she turned around to face him, "don't you find it at all suspicious that when we tell all these families a psychopath is after their children, instead of running to the greatest convergence of tatùs in the world, an organization sworn to protect, they're all running the other direction? On that note, don't you find it a little bit strange that all these people are in hiding to begin with?"

Devon shifted uncomfortably, shoving his hands deep in his pockets. "The Council thinks it's doing what's right, Rae. I mean—you saw what Camille can do. They make these laws for a reason."

"I thought they made Guilder for that reason." Rae pressed her lips tight before saying in a soft voice, "What about me? What about what I can do? You said it yourself, I'd be a Class Five. And all these laws you're praising, they're set in place to keep people like me from ever being born. The PC want me locked up and put in a safe place."

He glanced at the ground, avoiding her eyes. "I'm not praising their laws, I'm—"

"You're upholding them."

His eyes flashed up to meet hers. "I'm *breaking* them. Every day, I'm breaking them, Rae."

"But we're working for the company that put them in place. That forced this family," she gestured in the house, "to flee France and move to freaking Texas. That's who we work for, Dev."

"Well, what's the alternative?"

That was the question, wasn't it?

Rae turned back to the trees, locking her eyes on the horizon. What about Simon Kerrigan? She wished she had more of her father's journals. He had felt he didn't fit in to Guilder or the Privy Council. Did he have solid reasons for that? Or was he a lunatic like Cromfield? Rae sighed. "I don't know, Devon. I don't know..."

Chapter 7

Early the next morning, Rae, Devon, Molly, and Julian piled into the Escalade and headed out of town. They followed behind the Lachaises as far as the city limits before splitting off in opposite directions. While Camille and her family were heading to New York, Rae and her friends were off to the chilly beaches of San Francisco. The Lachaises were positive, and not afraid of moving on. It impressed Rae and gave her hope for the future—the near future, not the one where she was never going to die and Devon would grow old without her ever aging.

They didn't have a strict reason to go to San Fran. After Julian's 'episode' at the airport food court, he had yet to get another big-picture kind of vision. He could still see the things, the day to day results of his friends' decisions, but when it came to Cromfield, it was like he had hit a wall. The future was blocked. Hence, San Francisco. While it might not be the next place Cromfield was heading, it was the closest location on the list to where they were, and they could get there the fastest. Hopefully along the way, Julian's visions would kick back into gear in time for the next hybrid.

They made it as far as Yuma, Arizona before deciding to turn in for the night. Unfortunately, there had to be some kind of huge sports event or national disaster or something, because every hotel they passed was fully booked. Rae was finally able to secure them a single room in the shabbiest-looking motel any of them had ever seen by promising, through batted eyelashes, that they would pay double and be out first thing in the morning.

That still left the four of them utterly exhausted in a roach-filled hovel with a single bed.

There wasn't a sound as their eyes locked on the solitary mattress. A silent competition was formed in an instant, and each of them cast each other appraising looks as they inched closer.

"Well, I think it's clear that Rae and I should get the bed," Devon said shortly. "That way, at least two of us can use it. Instead of just one. Besides, I'm still recovering from a really bad head wound," he added unconvincingly.

"Oh, well that seems fair," Molly bristled. "*That's* the way the game is played? Just because you two happen to be screwing, you get the bed? In that case, I have an announcement to make. Julian and I have been secretly hooking up for the last few years, so I think we should get the bed."

"Speak for yourself," Julian muttered, eyeing the stains on mattress doubtfully. "I don't think I want to go anywhere near that thing."

"Can't you just conjure two other beds?" Devon asked Rae hopefully.

She shook her head. "Sure I could conjure them, but I couldn't un-conjure them when we were done. How would we explain that to the manager?"

"To be honest, I don't think the guy would notice," Molly said truthfully. "He seemed pretty concerned with his video games, and your money. That was about it."

"How about this," Devon said peaceably, "Rae and I can have the bed, but she can conjure you guys some awesome sleeping bags and some of that Tempur-pedic foam. We can just toss it in the dumpster before we leave." Molly raised an angry finger, and he hastened to add, "And, in return, Jules and Molly can have the first two showers. I'm sure there's not going to be any hot water for more than that anyway."

Molly paused mid-breath, obviously torn between the prospect of a mattress and a hot shower, before finally rolling her eyes with a huff. "Fine. You guys can have the bed. But if I see a roach down there, I'm blasting it, no questions asked. And *I* get the first shower. Sorry, Jules," she added, casting him a sideways glance.

"No problem," he said good-naturedly. Then he tossed her a wink, "Hey, if we've really been sleeping together for the last few years, maybe I could just join you. Share the hot water, wash each other's backs..."

The laughter that followed this statement eased a good deal of the tension in the room as Molly skipped off to the bathroom and Rae got to work conjuring the fluffiest, most comfortable sleeping bags she could imagine. It actually turned out a lot better than she would have thought. In fact, one could argue the little foam nests she created were a lot better than the mattress. She conjured a thick cover for the bed itself, anything to shield her and Devon from whatever ominous diseases lay beneath, and ended by installing an air freshener by the front door.

When Molly finally got out of the shower, she looked around curiously as she climbed into her bed. "Why does it smell like vanilla cookies?"

"Because of your handy best friend," Rae answered with a grin. "Why? Do you want a cookie?" She opened her palm and one appeared. "I'm getting really good at this!"

Molly took a bite and spat it right back out into the trash can. "Yeah...really good."

"Molls," Julian called from the bathroom, turning on the water for his own shower, "do you really have to leave your bra hanging up like this over the mirror? It's...kinda distracting."

"Yes I do—it cost eighty quid. That's a $150 American dollar bra!" she fired back. "It simply doesn't do to fold it up; it'll get weird creases."

"...are those rhinestones?"

"Stop looking at my bra, Julian."

"Sorry."

Less than a minute later, Julian also emerged from the bathroom, looking rather cross. Apparently, there had only been enough hot water for one shower. He settled onto his bed in a huff, shaking out his wet hair and shivering.

"What do you think, Rae?" Devon muttered with a tired yawn. "You want to try for one?"

"A shower?" she asked.

Julian shook his head. "I wouldn't."

Rae and Devon shared a quick look before she shook her head with a shrug and settled down on the bed. Despite the brilliant foam she'd created, the hard springs of the mattress still managed to cut through, and she couldn't for the life of her seem to fall asleep.

Devon, on the other hand, was out like a light the second his head touched the pillow. She watched him sleeping for what seemed like hours, trying to match his slow, calming breaths with her own. He looked so peaceful this way. So calm and undamaged. She realized with a dull ache that it was the only time he did anymore. Her eyes drifted around the room to where Molly was twitching sparks in her sleep, and Julian...? Well, it looked like Julian was having some kind of nightmare.

His entire face was tense and grimacing, and he kept jerking his head like he was trying to get away from something, but something wasn't letting him go. When the telltale stream of blood started trickling down his face, Rae leapt to her feet in alarm.

Taking care to not wake the others, she tiptoed past them and knelt beside Julian's makeshift bed. He looked different in his sleep, too—older, more guarded. The exact opposite of Devon.

"Jules," she shook him softly, "Julian, wake up."

He flinched away from her touch, but his eyes remained closed. She tried again, shaking him a little harder this time.

"Julian! You're having a nightmare. Wake up."

With a start, his eyes shot open and he pulled himself up. His lean, muscular arms were shaking as they held him up, and his face was about as pale as Rae had ever seen it.

She put a calming hand on his back as he tried to gather his wits. "Were you dreaming?" she asked quietly. "Or were you having a vision? It looked like you were having a nightmare..."

He gasped softly, trying to steady himself as she rubbed calming circles on his back.

"A nightmare...right."

They sat there for a while, neither speaking, neither knowing quite what to do. This was unfamiliar ground for the two of them. Rae considered Julian to be one of her closest friends. The fact was that he was hiding something—whatever it was she had seen in his thoughts—and now he was avoiding her so as not to talk about it. She didn't know what to do with that.

"Do you think you can fall back to sleep?" she finally asked. He glanced at her for a moment, then shook his head. "Come on," she said, helping him up. "Let's go for a walk."

It was a concert, Rae discovered, that's was filling up the town. She and Julian walked slowly down the street, hands buried in the pockets of two jackets she'd just conjured, listening to the roar of the crowd from a nearby stadium. It had to be some kind of country star, a type of music she truthfully couldn't abide, and, after sharing a quick glance with Julian, they started walking the other way.

They must have gone a good two miles before she finally tried to start up a conversation. "So...got any big plans for the summer?"

He stared at her incredulously for a second before bursting into laughter. She took one look at his shining, handsome face before laughing herself.

This was the Julian she knew and loved. *This* was the Julian she could talk to.

"I'm thinking I might learn Flemish," he said casually.

"Flemish, really?" She slipped into Sarah's tatù, finding she already knew how to speak it perfectly. "Well, I could give you some lessons if you like."

"That'd be great. You know, I may also take up chess. Or knitting."

She snorted with laughter and laced her arm through his. "I could see you as a knitter."

He nodded gravely. "I'd take it very seriously. And I'd only do it for the money. I hear there's big money in those little cardigan creations. I was thinking a whole tiny-dog line. Maybe open the line up to hamsters, gerbils, snakes."

"Jules..." She pulled him to a stop. There was a smile still lingering on her face, but she sobered up the longer she looked at him. "What exactly did I see inside your head? What're you not telling me?"

At once, he went pale as a sheet, shifting away from her and shivering in the cold. "I'm not. I don't know what you're talking about."

"Julian," she leaned forward persistently, "it's *me*."

His eyes tightened but he shook his head. "It's not important, Rae. It's not your problem."

She put her hands on her hips. "It's important enough that you're hiding it from—"

"I'm not *hiding* anything, I just..." He shivered again. "I just don't know what's going on."

They sat down on the curb and she took his hand, eyes silently encouraging him to continue.

"It's like Devon said. There's no way Cromfield can be aware of my presence. That's not how the gift works. It's impossible. Like, here—" he held his hands behind his back, "use my tatù, tell me which hand I'm going to open."

Rae's eyes screwed up as she concentrated. Aside from her father's and Ellie's, Julian's tatù was hands-down the most difficult she'd ever encountered. She was ashamed to say that most of the time she completely ignored it. It was hard to figure out, let alone progress with, and he was years ahead of her on its use. Plus, he was always around anyway.

"The left?"

He nodded. "But it doesn't matter. What matters is I couldn't feel you looking. You weren't inside my head. But, I... Rae, I can *feel* him watching me. I know he is. I don't know how it's possible, but I know he is." They were quiet for a second before he looked up suddenly. "You felt it, too, didn't you? When you were in my thoughts?"

Rae nodded slowly, almost relieved to finally get her unsettling time in Julian's visions out in the open. "I think I did. I'm pretty sure I felt it, too. When he looked up at the airport in Dallas... Jules, I felt like he was looking right at me."

Julian's face tightened as he looked out at the darkened city. "I knew it! That's exactly what I thought, too. And then when he looked at me..."

Rae's jaw dropped open as all at once it clicked. "That's when you had that fit at the airport!"

"It was like he was trying to force his way into my head." Julian's eyes dropped down to the ground. "Pry it open, or something. I've never felt anything like it before in my life. I thought it might kill me."

They were quiet again for a long time, just sitting on the curb, soaking in the implications of what was going on. Then, instead of the usual compassionate reaction that might have followed his admission, Rae's eyes shot up and she smacked him in the chest. Hard.

"*Shit*! What the hell, Kerrigan?!"

"How could you not have told me? Or Devon? Or Molly? Or literally anyone in the freaking world, Julian? How could you have kept something like that to yourself?"

His eyes dropped and his voice grew very small. "You would've stopped me. You wouldn't have let me keep going if you knew how bad it was."

"You're damn right!"

"But I have to keep going," he said softly. "There are people's lives at stake—"

"No. You have no right to be so brave with yourself. We are not going to do this if it's going to put you in danger."

He sighed, squeezing her hand despite her hard tone. "We're all in danger, Rae. And the longer this psycho is on the loose with the Privy Council not doing a thing about it, the more people are going to get hurt."

"Hey—look at me." She grabbed his face and turned it towards her. "*You are not going to be one of those people,* do you understand me?"

There was a moment's pause before he flashed her a sad grin and nodded. "Yes, ma'am."

She studied him for a second, testing his sincerity, before nodding herself. "Good." She linked their arms together again, bouncing back and forth to keep warm. "Now, let's get inside. I'm freezing!"

He chuckled, leading them back to the motel. "Can't you just conjure a space heater or something?"

She fixed a smile on her face, but tuned out of the conversation, replaying his words over and over again in her mind.

'I've never felt anything like it before in my life. I thought it might kill me.'

She shuddered and gripped his arm tighter in her own.

Not if she had anything to say about it.

They got to San Francisco at around six o'clock the next evening. It was the perfect time to get there, because people were just coming home from work, and, according to Julian's memories of Cromfield's files, this guy, Benjamin Mills, was supposed to be some kind of computer wizard. They pulled up just as he was walking back into his apartment tower. Lanky, horn-rimmed glasses, clutching a bag of groceries in his hand, he couldn't be missed.

Molly smiled to herself as she climbed out of the car. "Oh...I've got this one."

Rae waved her off with a grin as the boys glanced at each other with twin scowls.

"That'll never work," Julian scoffed.

Devon nodded self-righteously. "I don't know what sort of stereotype you girls are working from, but guys are not universally easy. It's not like he's going to invite her in, just like..." His voice trailed off as Molly waved excitedly from the curb, arm in arm with Benjamin.

"I'm sorry," Rae smirked as she pushed open her door, "you were saying?"

Benjamin Mills didn't just live on the top floor of the apartment complex—he *owned* the top floor of the apartment complex. Rae glanced around the lush penthouse with a stifled sigh, wishing very much that she could get back to London to a penthouse of her own.

"So...you guys all have ink, like Miss Skye?" he asked eagerly.

Rae raised her eyebrows and looked at her friend; the friend who was clearly enjoying all the attention. *Miss Skye*? "Uh—yeah, we do. But it's not having a tatù that's the problem," she said, knowing this is where she came in. She lifted the back of her shirt, "It's having two."

Benjamin's jaw dropped open as he knelt down on the floor to get a closer look at the design. His fingers reached out automatically to trace it, and Devon caught him by the hand. "Okay, buddy—that's close enough."

"I'm sorry," Benjamin said quickly, scrambling to his feet. "It's just—I've never seen another hybrid before. It's incredible! And you work for this Privy Council?"

"Yeah, we all do," Rae answered. "Except...*this* mission isn't really sanctioned."

"You see, Benny, the PC aren't the only ones interested in hybrids," Molly continued. "There's a man coming. A very bad man who means you harm. We came here to warn you."

Without a second's pause, the four friends launched into the 'Cromfield Dissertation,' just as they always did. They watched the telltale progression of signs across Benjamin's face. The curiosity, astonishment, realization, and finally—fear.

Only...Benjamin didn't quite get to that last one.

"Well, I wish him the best of luck," he laughed when they were all done. "Let me tell you something; if this Cromfield guy can get through my multi-million-dollar security system, then he can take what he wants."

Rae blinked. This was usually the part where the hybrids ran. "I don't think you understand exactly what we're telling you," she said slowly. "This guy isn't going to be impressed with a bunch of fancy gadgets and an expensive locked door. These are tatùs we're talking about. It's basically magic. He's somehow outfoxed hundreds of hybrids over the last few centuries, so, if you want to stand a chance, you're going to have to—"

"But that's what's so great about it," Benjamin extended his arm and rolled up his sleeve, "my tatù *is* a bunch of fancy gadgets."

The ink on his arm was of a single lightbulb, so bright it seemed to illuminate the rest of his skin. But Rae sensed there was a bit more to it than met the eye.

"It's a fusion, right?" he gushed. "Intuition and technology. Paired together," he gestured to the hundreds of prototypes and half-finished machines littering his luxury suite. "Well, needless to say, it got me this penthouse."

Rae sniffed self-importantly. She wouldn't call him more than a Class Two.

Devon, always the patient one, the one to convince everyone what needed to be done and why, said, "And that's really great for you. But this guy Cromfield doesn't care. He wants to study you, experiment with your gift. He's been doing it for hundreds of years, and, trust me, we've seen the pictures; No one makes it out alive."

Benjamin was completely unfazed. "Do you see these cameras?" He pointed to several tiny lights blinking all over the apartment. "This is a state-of-the-art security system. I designed it myself. All the feed can hook up to any computer, tablet, or cellular device anywhere in the world. That means that if anyone were to come in here uninvited, I'd get an email, a text, a call. I'd basically get a bunch of carrier pigeons knocking on my window, telling me it wasn't safe." He laughed loudly at his own joke, then quieted down quickly when he saw the four stoic faces staring back at him. "So, really," he muttered in a far demurer tone, "thank you for your concern, but I'll be just fine."

"Benny," Molly tried again, "you're not hearing what we're—"

"I'm not going anywhere," he cut her off suddenly. Apparently, the possibility of a threat against his person had managed to cool even the startling passion he'd developed for Miss Skye.

"Look," Devon tried to ease the sudden tension, "we really can't, in good conscience, leave you here alone. It's not a matter of *if*; it's a matter of *when*. And with your tatù, as technologically brilliant as it might be, you're not going to have anything to fight him off."

"It's Devon, isn't it?" Benjamin sneered.

Devon nodded.

"I'm not trying to tell you how to do your job, so please don't lecture me on the security of this penthouse, when I designed it myself. Now, I promise you, if anything happens to me, I'll program the device to give you a call right away. But until then, I want you to get the hell off my property."

Rae's eyebrows shot into her hair. "You're really throwing us—"

"*Out. Now.* Before I call security."

Five minutes later, they were standing out on the street. They stared at each other blankly, at a complete loss as to what to do, until a passing cab sprayed them all awake with a giant puddle.

"Gross..." Molly muttered, shaking off her hands.

"I can't believe this!" Rae exclaimed. "He's really going to just...hope for the best?"

"Will Cromfield come here next?" Devon asked Julian. "Is this guy about to die, or what?"

Rae shot Julian a look, but said nothing as he tried to scan the immediate future. She hadn't yet had an opportunity to talk to the others about what was happening, but at this second, it didn't seem to much matter. According to Julian, he'd been effectively shut out of Cromfield's head since he landed in Dallas.

His eyes glassed over momentarily before he shook his head. "It's all blank; I can't see. Maybe if we tried—"

All at once, he fell to his knees with an excruciating cry. The passing pedestrians gave him a wide berth as his hands came up to his temples, ready to tear them apart.

"Julian!" Rae dropped down beside him, already conjuring the morphine in her hand. "Get out of there!"

Devon shot her a strange look, but, before he could say anything, Julian opened his eyes with a gasp. His face was shocking white, and another steady stream of blood was dripping down his chin.

"What is it?" Devon asked gravely. "Is Benjamin about to die?"

In the blink of an eye, Julian leapt to his feet, still trying to catch his breath, but ready to go.

"No...but someone else is!"

Chapter 8

"Julian! Slow down!"

Even using their tatùs, Rae and Devon could barely keep up with him as he raced through the airport to the front desk. Molly, whose legs were half the size of everyone else's and had no supernatural support, lagged behind, Except for her voice. That carried loud and clear throughout the airport.

"You don't understand—we *have* to hurry!" he cried, pushing people out of his way as he cut shamelessly in line to the front. "We need to get there *now*; this guy's going to be killed!" he hissed only loud enough for someone with a particular fennec fox tatù would catch. Rae had slipped into Devon's ability the moment Julian took off.

Rae and Deon crashed in behind him, in a breathless heap as he hopped up on the counter and summoned the attention of a middle-aged booking attendant. Julian was lucky he was so good-looking—anyone else would probably have been asked to leave. Except probably Devon. Sexy, good-looking, and a lovely accent seemed to be a winner most times these days.

The attendant just smoothed down her skirt and sauntered over, giving him a seductive smile. "Can I help you, sweetie?"

"Yes!" He ran his hands manically back through his hair, completely oblivious to her intentions. "I need four tickets to Japan, to leave as soon as possible."

Rae turned to Devon in alarm and mouthed, *Japan?*

The attendant's smile cooled a bit as she began typing. "Tokyo, Osaka, or Fukuoka?"

For the first time since Julian had had the vision, his pace slowed as he faltered. "Oh...uh..."

Sensing the problem, Devon stepped forward and distracted the woman with a throwaway question while Julian looked down at the floor, covering his eyes with his hand. A second later, his head snapped back up with a triumphant shine.

Devon shot the attendant a sexy smile. "So they have you do that *every* time you check a bag—"

"Osaka!" Julian declared proudly, slamming his hand down on the counter and making everyone jump. "Four tickets to Osaka, please."

Molly caught up to them, only to be immediately whisked away in the opposite direction toward the boarding gates.

The second the four of them were through security—invisibly jumping over the barriers just like before—Devon crossed his arms over his chest and turned to Julian with a pointed stare. "Okay...what the hell is going on here? First you collapse, then *you*..." he fixed Rae with the same piercing eyes, "...seem to know something about it I don't, and now we're going to Japan?"

"There's a man there. A businessman. Mid-forties. Suit and briefcase. His name's Akihiro Nakano. And at eleven-forty, the morning of the twenty-eighth, he's going to die," Julian said all of this in a strange robotic monotone as the others stared at each other in alarm.

Devon opened his mouth, but failed to speak many times before he finally managed, "You got all that from one vision? Not just where Cromfield was going, but what he was actually going to—"

"This vision wasn't like any of the others." Julian's face still had that adrenaline-fueled sheen to it, and his eyes seemed to be having trouble focusing on just one thing. "It was crystal clear. I could see every detail, hear every sound. I could smell the noodles in the restaurant down the street." He pushed Devon into a chair in the patio section of a terminal bar and grill as the girls settled themselves beside them. "Cromfield walks up to him outside a coffee shop and shoots him right in the stomach. No questions asked. I saw a newspaper lying on one of the tables and got the date. It's going to happen, Devon. And we need to get there before it does."

Devon nodded slowly, watching his friend with steady, albeit worried, eyes. "Okay...then we'll get there before Cromfield does." He glanced around to make sure no one was listening except the four of them. Satisfied, he leaned his head toward Julian and Rae. "But enough of this crap! I want you to tell me right now what's going on with your visions! And if you say 'nothing' or blow me off, I swear on everything good, Jules—I'll kick your ass." He pressed his finger up against Rae's mouth, as she was about to speak. "I'll whup yours, too, if I have to, sweetheart."

Julian's dark eyes flashed to Rae for help, and she leaned diplomatically away from Devon's finger. "We think that...Cromfield has somehow been made aware of Julian's presence in his mind."

Devon and Molly blinked in unison. "*What*?!"

"When I used Carter's gift to find out about Texas, and relived Julian's vision for myself, there was a moment when I was positive Cromfield looked me. Right at me, not just in my general direction. I mean, *him*—I mean...you know what I mean."

Molly shook her head in quick confusion. "I thought that was impossible."

"It *is* impossible. It's like looking into the future when we aren't even there," Devon said slowly, his eyes flicking to Julian. "Jules, are you sure?"

Julian's cheeks paled, but he nodded firmly. "I have no clue how, or why, it's even possible, but I'm sure. It isn't the first time I'd gotten that impression, but it was definitely the strongest." He inhaled sharply, his next words coming out fast, as if he didn't want to admit to it, "And immediately after, he turned it around on me. It was like he was trying to break his way into my head." A sharp breath hissed from Julian. "And I couldn't stop him. He was too strong." Rae could see his hands shaking, whether from fear or frustration, or maybe both, she wasn't sure.

Devon sank down a couple inches in his chair before running his fingers up through his hair with a sigh.

Rae took his other hand under the table and squeezed. "What is it, Dev?"

He closed his eyes and shook his head. "I can't believe I'm saying this right now, but do you know who I wish was here?"

A sinking feeling hung heavy in Rae's gut. "Who?" she whispered.

"Carter."

The three friends glanced at each other quickly before looking away. At some point during the last few weeks, each one of them had felt the same way. How nice it would be to have an adult in this crazy situation with them; have an adult shouldering some of the responsibility and coming up with a plan. They'd never realized how much it meant to have someone looking out for them and calling the shots, until that person was out of the picture. Carter was their go-to. Of all the teachers and instructors and parent figures, he was the one who'd had the most faith in him. There was a reason he was the president of the Privy Council and the headmaster of Guilder.

"I know," Rae said softly. "I do, too."

"He would know what to say," Devon muttered. "He would know if there was some kind of precedent for this..." He huffed in frustration. "Carter would know what to do."

"Well it sounds like whether there's a precedent or not, it's definitely happening. Cromfield knows we're on to him," Molly said glumly. "And it kind of makes sense. Remember how I have this awesome kind of connection with Noah because we share the same tatù? And how I just knew that Mr. Padron had it, too?" She stared at Julian with a hint of pity in her eyes. "I mean,

Jules, Cromfield had an entire room of the exact same pictures you'd been drawing for months..."

"I know," Julian shivered, "that's when I wondered about it for the first time. I never said anything, but I should have." He sighed, frustrated and at his wit's end.

"Well, one thing's for sure: you're certainly never watching him again," Devon said firmly, glaring around as if he expected resistance. "There is *no way* we're going to let you keep doing this if this is the kind of risk you're talking about. I don't care what you think you have to—"

"Dev?" Julian cut him off with a small smile. "Your girlfriend beat you to it last night."

Devon's eyes landed on Rae, innocently twiddling her thumbs, before he sank back in his chair, looking a little deflated. "Oh."

'Now boarding...Flight 871 to Kansai Airport...Calling all first-class passengers...'

"That's us." Julian smiled, trying to sound encouraging. "It's going to be fine. We're all going to be fine. We're going to stop that bastard, Cromfield, and the Privy Council is going to make us kings and queens of Narnia." He shrugged. "Or whatever."

As they got to their feet, Molly reached over and gave Julian an unexpected hug. "Just try to keep it together on the plane, alright? Cromfield doesn't control you. I know you're not a victim. Your head is your own property, no one else's. If you don't want someone to touch it, they can't. Stand up for yourself. Break the cycle. No means no. You don't have to—"

"Molls?" He put a hand on her shoulder with a smile. "I get it. Thanks."

It wasn't until she walked away with a watery smile that Rae noticed the PSA poster for teen drinking mounted on the wall behind her. She elbowed Devon, and nodded in the direction of the poster. He grinned, but managed to keep his mouth shut as Julian walked by.

While Julian's 'food court confession' had temporarily alleviated everyone's nerves, they came back in full force as they sat on the incredibly long flight across the Pacific. According to Devon's calculations, they would land in Osaka with about forty minutes to find whatever little coffee shop Julian had seen in the vision. Needless to say, every little detail helped, and they spent endless hours recounting everything he had seen: from the street numbers, to the advertisements, to the types of clothing the pedestrians were wearing.

Rae was called upon many times to translate something in Japanese, but, in the end, it was to no avail. There were just too many places where it could possibly be.

As fate would have it, it was random chance that pointed them in the right direction.

"Excuse me?" a young Japanese woman tapped Rae on the shoulder.

Rae turned around in surprise, and the girl's eyes temporarily glazed over as Devon and Julian followed suit on either side. Rae resisted the urge to roll her eyes at the handsome dudes beside her. "Um...yes? Can I help you with something?"

"I'm sorry to interrupt. I know it's kinda rude. It's just...you all have been talking for a long time and I couldn't help but overhear." She smiled apologetically. "You say you're looking for a coffee shop next to a skating rink in Osaka? Well, I don't know about the coffee shop, but there are only three skating rinks in the city, and two of them are closed down at the moment. You want the one on the south end. I can give you the streets."

"Really?" Rae blinked in surprise.

She smiled. "Really. My friends and I go there all the time." She must have misinterpreted the blank looks of astonishment on their faces entirely, and backtracked as fast as she could. "I'm sorry; I didn't mean to be eavesdropping. It's just, you said it was life or death. Maybe it's not..."

"No! It is! I mean, it's not. It's, uh... Well, thank you. Thank you so much!" Rae exclaimed, wondering if it would be weird if she gave the girl a hug through the chairs. "It totally *is* life or death, we...we really like skating," she finished rather lamely, wishing she had come up with something better to say.

The girl smiled shyly and wrote down some symbols on a napkin, passing it through the slit in the chair.

Rae translated them immediately in her head. "Thank you so much, really!" she thanked the girl again before turning back around to her friends. "This is incredible! We can just call a cab from the airport and go right there." Maybe Fate didn't want Cromfield messing with its plans either.

"See, Jules!" Molly nudged him cheerfully. "You're saving this guy's life."

Julian took an unsteady breath. "Yeah, *or*, if we hit any traffic, we're going to get there just in time to see him get shot to death." His friends paused uncertainly, and he shook his head with a tired sigh. "I'm sorry, I'm just...I'm going to be really glad when this goose-chase is over."

"Me, too." Rae leaned back in her chair. "Worst mission ever."

"It's not a mission," Devon mumbled.

"We're already halfway through the names on our list," Molly said, with more forced enthusiasm than she obviously felt. "It won't be that much longer now—"

"I'm sorry," Devon interjected, "am I the only one who's not terribly excited to be going back to London?"

The other three turned to him in surprise.

"Why would you say that?" Rae asked.

Devon raised his eyebrows. "Do you guys have any idea what we're going to be going back to? Do you have any idea how much trouble we're going to be in with Carter? With the Privy Council? With your *mother*?" he added.

Rae stifled a shudder—a truly terrifying prospect.

Devon must have thought facing Rae's mom might be worst for him as well. "It's certainly not going to be rainbows and sunshine." He shrugged. "That's all I'm saying."

For the first time since takeoff, it was perfectly quiet in Row 3. The four friends sat with their eyes fixed on the seats in front of them, worlds away as they wondered how each of their particular familial situations would implode the second they got back to England.

The plane had already begun its descent by the time Molly leaned across Rae, and slapped Devon suddenly in the chest with a vicious glare.

He jumped in his seat; she'd apparently used quite some voltage, and he turned to her in bewilderment. "What the hell was that for?" he demanded, twitching slightly from the shock.

"What was it for?" she chanted back sarcastically. "It was for your damn all-encompassing negativity, that's what it was for."

Rae and Julian started laughing behind their hands as Molly and Devon had the stare-off of a lifetime.

Molly frowned at him. "You keep those thunderclouds to yourself, Wardell. If you don't, *I'll* bring the lightning." She leaned back slowly, still shooting him threatening looks as he dissolved in laughter with the rest of them.

"Tell me the truth," Rae asked as they touched down. "How long have you been waiting to say that?"

"Oh, my gosh, Rae!" Molly smoothed back her hair with an intensely-satisfied expression. "You have no idea!"

The second they landed in Osaka, that same kind of frantic kinetic energy overtook each of them in turn as they left their bags in the terminal and darted to the cab service. They hopped into the nearest one they could, barreling right past what looked like a pair of honeymooners, and threw all their newly exchanged currency over the barrier. Rae barked the directions in Japanese, and the next second they were off.

So this is Japan, Rae thought as she stared out the window. Was there ever going to be a time when she'd get to see one of these extraordinary countries under normal circumstances? When they weren't looking down the barrel of a gun? Would she and Devon ever get to vacation together? Did the Privy Council allow for such carefree time off? More importantly, when they got back to England, was the Privy Council ever going to let them off the titanium leash they'd surely be putting around each of their necks?

As they pulled up to the coffee shop, everything appeared exactly as Julian had described it. The buildings, the weather, everything. All the concerns of England vanished from Rae's head, replaced with a single thought: Where the hell was Akihiro Nakano?

They settled themselves at an outdoor restaurant across the street, watching the café with eyes peeled, each of them checking their watches on a steady basis. If Cromfield was going to indeed walk up from the northern sidewalk, as Julian had predicted, they would be able to see him coming a mile away.

Julian's foot was bouncing nervously under the table as he checked his watch for the twentieth time in the past five minutes. "Eleven thirty-eight. Just two more minutes," he murmured. The bouncing increased. "This is so weird; everything is exactly how I saw it. Look—that guy's about to sneeze."

Devon turned to Rae. "So you know the plan?"

"As soon as we see Cromfield, I turn invisible and knock him down. Meanwhile, you and Jules get Nakano to cover, while Molly provides cover fire. We meet back at the skating rink."

Devon raised his eyebrows sternly. "*And?*"

Rae rolled her eyes. "*And* under no circumstances am I to engage Cromfield. I'm simply knocking him off balance to give you guys the chance to give him the slip."

All at once, Julian straightened up, his eyes locking across the street like a hawk. "That's him!" He breathed sharply. "That's Akihiro."

They watched as a middle-aged businessman walked out of the coffee shop, blinking in the bright afternoon sun. He stretched out his arms, spilling a few drops of his coffee, before lifting his hand to call a cab.

As one, their eyes scanned up and down the roads, searching for Cromfield.

Julian said he had simply walked up? He'd have to be walking very fast; the final minute was almost over and Nakano was set to die at precisely eleven-forty.

"Jules?" Devon asked nervously.

Julian leaned forward, not even breathing, when it suddenly happened.

The minute passed.

He straightened up like someone had slapped him. "What? I...I don't..."

Nakano's cab arrived and he climbed inside, easing away into traffic.

The three friends shared a quick look before turning as one to Julian.

"I don't understand," Julian fumed. "I saw this happen. I SAW it! One minute ago, I *saw* this man die. How could...?"

Rae got to her feet, a sudden sinking feeling weighing heaving her chest. A moment later, she opened her hand and a cell-phone appeared in her palm. Going off memory, she typed in the number listed for Benjamin Mills and waited. On the third ring, a deep voice answered.

A voice that was certainly not that of Benjamin Mills...

Chapter 9

"Kon'nichiwa!"

Rae froze. Every inch of her stood rooted to the ground and the air around her stilled.

It wasn't the voice she had been expecting. Not the one she had been dreading. The one that slithered around behind her, from her waking hours to her darkest dreams. Soundless, toneless, ever present. A distant echo of terrible things to come.

This was something else entirely.

It wasn't the voice of a villain. There were no dark rumblings or a sinister hiss. He sounded...pleasant. Engaging. And thoroughly delighted to be talking to her.

"Crom—" she cleared her throat and hissed, "Cromfield. Jeremiah Cromfield."

On the sidewalk across from her, Molly, Devon, and Julian rotated slowly around, stiffening like three horrified statues. The world behind them rushed on in a streak of people and lights, completely oblivious to what was happening. But the four of them were frozen in time, barely breathing as they waited.

Cheerful laughter crackled through the static, and Rae pressed the phone harder to her ear. *This can't be happening. This has got to be a bad dream or something.* Rae's brain couldn't think or process. She could only stare into the eyes of her friends, unable to do anything else.

"Indeed it is, my dear! Indeed, it is! I just can't tell you how happy I am to be hearing your lovely voice! When I had this vision yesterday—saw that you would be calling—I have to admit I got a little nervous. I've been waiting so long. And me, nervous?" He laughed again. "For the first time in over a hundred years. Can you imagine?!"

He laughed again and Rae shuddered.

Breaking out of his trance, Devon held up a furious hand and took a step forward, mouthing, *Hang up the phone, Rae!*

"No, sweet Rae, you're not going to hang up the phone," the voice on the other end grew softer, more menacing. "You can tell that impatient boy-toy of yours to take a step back and wait his turn. You and I are going to have a conversation. I'm entitled to it."

Fingers trembling, Rae held up her hand, motioning for Devon to stop. There were tears in her eyes and she shook all over, but knew she had to keep listening. There was something deep inside her that wasn't letting her hang up the phone. Something she didn't quite understand. Fear? She'd lived a life of fear, but this... this she couldn't explain.

"Of course, one can *almost* understand Dear Devon's impatience," Cromfield continued. "After all, he only has a few short decades left with you, if he lives that long. Whereas you and I, oh, sweet Rae, we have the rest of eternity."

Rae's eyes flicked up and met Devon's gaze in silence. Even from where he was standing, he could easily hear every word. It was as if there was a sudden dimming in his bright eyes, a strange deadening she could feel reflected in her own.

"But enough about that silly boy! Let's talk more about you!" Cromfield said in the same enthusiastic voice as before. "You've followed my little trail of breadcrumbs all over the world, you clever girl! I must admit, as much as it's inconvenienced me, I'm actually rather proud of you. What's a few lost hybrids here and there?" He laughed, the sound turning more evil as the seconds passed. "You're the only one I want."

Rae just shook her head, unable to speak, unable to hang up; simply stuck as hordes of people strode by her, standing in a horrified daze as the man who ruined her entire life tried to strike up a friendly conversation.

"Now, Rae, you wouldn't happen to be in Japan, would you?" The laugh that followed this time was mocking.

It was those words that finally snapped her out of her trance. She looked up with sudden passion as her eyes locked on Julian's petrified face. "Where's Benjamin Mills?" she hissed.

"Benny?" Cromfield laughed. "Oh, he's fine! He's washing up; we just got back from a delightful dinner. You wouldn't believe some of the ingenious ideas that man has running around his little head. Delightful!"

"If you—"

"Is there something you'd like to say to him?" Cromfield cut her off. "I'd be happy to take a message." He was just playing with her now, keeping her on the line as he did as he pleased. Just like he'd always done as he pleased, her entire life; uprooting it as he saw fit, taking her parents out of the equation. Leaving her ignorant as to who she was, *what* she was until a time of his choosing.

Her teeth ground together, incensed beyond belief, but, when she spoke, it was in surprisingly pleasant tones. "Dear Jeremiah!" She let the word hang in between them, and heard a sharp intake of breath on the other end.

A few paces away, Devon's face tightened as though she'd stabbed him.

Rae winked at Devon. She could flippin' play Cromfield's game. "I don't want you to hurt Benjamin. If you hurt him, you hurt me."

There was a profound pause on the other end of the line before, "Rae, I would never do anything to hurt you. I would burn the world to the ground before I let that happen."

Yeah, you'd never do anything to hurt me except kill my father, kidnap my mother, essentially orphan me, and threaten the lives of everyone I meet. Cool. Thanks. I owe you one.

"But you have to understand the significance of what I'm doing here. Not everyone was born with your unique gift, my sweet. I'm simply doing all I can to—" His voice cut off as another pair of footsteps entered the room. There was a muffling sound, and she could tell Cromfield had put his hand over the receiver. "Just a minute, Rae. Yes, you can pour us some drinks."

"Benjamin!" Rae screamed at the top of her lungs, but Cromfield was already walking into the next room where Benjamin couldn't hear her.

"Anyway, my dear, I've got to run. But it was a pleasure speaking with you today. A pleasure I hope to repeat again very soon. Send my love to the boyfriend and Miss Skye." He snapped his fingers, the sound echoing through the phone, making Rae jerk. "Oh, and if you wouldn't mind, thank Julian for me. His help has been truly invaluable over these last few days. I really couldn't have done it without him."

Rae's eyes locked onto Julian's dark ones, and, although he couldn't hear what Cromfield had said, his face paled and he began slowly shaking his head. "What have you been doing to him?" she whispered.

"*Doing* to him? Why, Rae, you make it sound so sinister! I've simply been watching him, the same way you had him watching me. How fortunate that one of your closest friends happens to be a twin tatù! It made getting to you know and your little group so much easier."

Rae thought of the look on Julian's face went he went down at the airport. He'd said it felt like someone was trying to pry their way into his head. It felt like it was killing him.

"There's Miss Skye, for example, your best friend; soon to be your roommate in your new London apartment. I really have to congratulate you on that, by the way; such a find! I also would have chosen the balcony with the park view. Then, of course, there's Devon, the temporary boyfriend," he sighed, as if the thought exasperated him.

Rae's eyes flashed up to Devon again, watching as he ground his jaw to a pulp, his hands periodically turning into fists.

"Talented, handsome, strong, and, despite his strict upbringing, still willing to break the rules of the Privy Council; willing to throw it all away for love. If we were talking about anyone other than you, Miss Kerrigan, I would have said it was a good match. In fact, if we were talking about anyone other than you, I might actually be very curious to see what sort of children such a match would provide. Alas, it isn't meant to be. All good things must come to an end."

Rae closed her eyes and gripped the phone in her fist. It felt like she was losing whatever this globe-hopping road trip had left of her sanity, falling into the darker recesses of her mind with no one to stop her. No end in sight. Just dark, hidden amongst the rays of the sun. "Stop," she begged in a quiet whisper.

But Cromfield was just getting warmed up. "And then there's Julian himself. Surprisingly a shy boy, especially considering the way everyone looks up to him. And what a gift! Although it pains me, I have to admit he's progressed with it so much faster than I did at his age. If he were also gifted with immortality, there's really no telling what he could do. But he simply won't have the time to discover all the little tricks I've picked up over the centuries, like how to plant a vision in someone else's head, for example. I doubt he'll ever master that."

Rae's voice caught in her throat. "How to...what do you mean, plant a vision?"

"Japan," Cromfield explained cheerfully. "Texas was a test, just a little run-through to make sure I could do it. Normally it wouldn't be so difficult, you see, but Julian shares my ability and has an especially resilient mind."

"Texas was a test?" Rae repeated, getting him back on point.

"Yes, an experiment. I wasn't planning on going to Texas next. In fact, I was on my way to Bolivia when I finally identified the presence that had been nagging away at my mind. An added consciousness adds weight, you know? Something I'm afraid your little friend is going to learn all too well. Anyway, I decided to see if I could reverse his little spy game, and give him an idea of my own. I showed him landing in Texas, and then watched to see where you would go. Sure enough, a few hours later you landed in Dallas."

We played right into his hands. Despite the busy pedestrian crowds, Rae sank to a crouch, her buckling knees refusing to support her a second longer. *We played right into his hands...*

"Of course, once I knew it could work, I had to do it again. This time I sent all of you to Japan. I'm sorry to have sent you flying off across the Pacific, my sweetheart, but you see, Mr. Mills has a gift of particular interest to me, and, as much as I'd like to indulge you, I simply couldn't let this one go."

Rae stood back up, breathing as though she'd just run a marathon. "*Indulge* me?"

"Speaking of which, I really mustn't keep him waiting a minute longer. You certainly do bring out the talker in me!" he chuckled benevolently. "I can't wait to finally see you in person, sweet-heart. We really have a lot to discuss. I've been dreaming about you for years and years."

"Rae," Devon growled. "Hang up the damn—"

She could almost hear Cromfield smile. "Goodbye now, love. Stay safe."

The line clicked off.

For a moment, a very long moment, the four of them just stood there. They were positioned strangely, not in their usual mixed group. It was three on one, the three of them staring back at her as if she'd just beamed down from outer space. Then a dry sob shook her thin shoulders, and Devon crossed the space in between them.

The next breath, she was in his arms, gasping for air as though for the entire conversation she'd been holding her breath. "I can't—" she said again and again. "I can't be here with him. We can't be the only ones left—"

Two large hands interrupted, pulled her abruptly from Devon's arms. She looked up in surprise to see Julian looking down at her, pale as a ghost.

"Is he... He's there with Mills right now, isn't he? In San Francisco?" He hadn't been able to hear the other side of the conversation like Devon had, but, based on Rae's disjointed questions, he had certainly assumed the worst. "He knew I was watching, he...he showed me Japan on purpose? To get us away from Mills?"

Rae's lips quivered and her eyes spilled over with tears.

Devon pulled her back to his chest as Julian sank into a nearby chair, looking absolutely gutted.

Molly sat down beside him, rubbing his back and murmuring, "You didn't know, you couldn't know."

Rae took advantage of their distraction to look up into Devon's eyes. "He's probably killing him right now. And it's my fault. He's doing all of this because he wants *me*. He's doing it to get to *me*!"

Devon took her hard by the shoulders. "That is *never* going to happen! Do you hear me?!"

"What can you do?!" she shrieked back, ignoring the people who'd stopped to stare at them. "He's right, Dev! In fifty or sixty years, you're going to die. You're all going to die, and I'm going to be all alone. Who's going to save me then?!"

Devon's mouth opened, but no words came out. He just stared back at her in helpless, furious rage; willing to give his life to set this right, but completely powerless to stop it.

A tortured cry cut through the silence that followed.

Rae and Devon whirled around to see Julian doubled over, clutching his head. Molly shrieked and grabbed him in a huge hug from behind, her little arms not even stretching halfway across his long ones.

"Rae! The morphine!"

Rae rushed forward, and Julian opened his eyes with a groan. "He's showing me," he panted painfully. "He's showing me everything he's doing. They're in the apartment now. He's drugging Benjamin's drink..."

His eyes closed again, and Rae held out her hand to create a syringe, her eyes blurring with tears as she shielded herself behind her long jacket. Much to her surprise, Devon reached into her pocket and grabbed the phone.

"What're you doing?" she demanded, turning around in fright. "Dev, you can't call him—"

"I'm calling Carter," he said shortly, waiting as the line rang. "It's what we should have done a long time ago."

A moment later, a distant yelling thundered through the phone. Devon winced and held it away from his head, but spoke up to try to make himself heard.

"I understand, but... Yes, I understand that, but... *sir*!"

The yelling finally paused.

"Cromfield's in a penthouse apartment on 4001 Mission Street in San Francisco, with a hybrid Class Three named Benjamin Mills. He's...sir, he's about to kill him."

Julian's head bowed in his hands and Rae rushed forward. "Sorry," she muttered, filling up the syringe with the clear liquid. "I forgot."

"No!" He flinched away from her. "Don't give it to me."

Rae and Molly shook their heads at the same time. "What?"

"I said, don't give it to me." His eyes burned as he grabbed the syringe from her hand and shattered it against the sidewalk. "If this guy dies, it's because of me. I don't deserve blinders now. If he dies, I'm going to watch the whole thing. Every second."

The girls exchanged worried looks, but Devon sighed behind them and Rae's attention turned immediately back to him. His head was bowed as he listened as Carter shouted at him. Rae quickly switched out of Ethan's tatù so she could listen herself.

"...trusted you a hell of a lot more than this, Devon! You and Julian were the ones I never had to worry about. And now this? Do you know how worried we've all been? Do you know the lies I've had to tell to the rest of the Council just to keep them off your back? At this point, the Council is the least of my problems!"

Devon's shoulders fell as his face tightened with remorse. "I know," he said softly. "I'm sorry. We were just trying to do what was right—"

"What was right?! You're a smart kid, Devon. Surely you didn't think for even a moment that you could do this whole thing on your own. What am I supposed to tell your father when he comes banging on my door for the millionth time today? And Beth?! Has Rae even thought about what this is doing to her—?"

With a gentle hum, Rae's body switched automatically into Charles' healing tatù, so she could hear no more. For a second, she was vaguely surprised. She usually had to make a bit more of a voluntary decision to do so. Her arms curled protectively around her chest, and she turned her head with a shaky sigh. Maybe her body knew something she didn't...

"Sir," Devon finally interrupted, looking to all the world like he'd just been stripped bare, "Benjamin Mills—"

"Yes, Wardell," Carter was shouting loud enough now that all of them could hear, even Julian and Molly. "I alerted dispatch the second you gave the address. Now you, Rae, Julian, and Molly are going to get your asses back to London at once. Do you hear me?! I want to see you on school grounds in the next twenty-four hours, or so help me—"

"We understand," Devon said quickly. "We'll get back straight away."

"Tell him thank you," Molly whispered, silent tears running down her face as well.

Devon hesitated. "And, sir? Thanks. We're sorry... Really."

"Sorry?" Carter laughed derisively. "Not as sorry as you're going to be the second you walk through these doors. In fact, I'm looking forward to making you particularly sorry myself, Devon."

The phone clicked off, and Devon stared at it for a moment before putting on his best face and turning to his friends. "Well...the cops are on their way. They should get to Mills' apartment any minute. Or tatù security. Whatever it takes." He ran his hand through his hair. "Jules?" He glanced at Julian questioningly.

But Julian just shook his head, looking like at any moment he might pass out. "He shut me out. I can't see any more. They'd just sat down for drinks."

"Then maybe it's not too late," Molly said hopefully. "Maybe they'll get there in time—"

"Of course it's too late," Julian glowered, his eyes burning a hole in the cement. "It was too late the second I got that damn vision and we set foot on the plane to Japan. He's going to—"

"*Hey!*" Devon clapped him hard on the shoulder, keeping a constant hand on Rae at the same time. "This is not your fault. You got a vision, you told us what it was, and we went. End of story."

Julian shook his head. "It's not that simple."

"*Make it that simple,*" Devon commanded, turning back to Rae. "Babe, I know what Carter said, but I feel like we have to—"

"—go back to San Francisco," Rae finished for him. She had been thinking the same thing. Whether or not the cops got to Mills in time, she needed to see it for herself. In a way, she felt like she needed to see it simply to prove that it was really happening. So far, this whole thing had felt like a bad dream. She needed to see it was real.

"Absolutely not," Molly protested quickly, still rubbing Julian's back. "We are in *so* much trouble as it is. We need to get back to London, pronto."

"No!" Julian interrupted, getting to his feet. "We need to go back. We need to see him. I'm the one who left him there, exposed. I need to go back."

"*We* left him," Rae corrected with sudden fierceness. "The only reason Cromfield is running around on this little crusade is so he and I can 'lead our people into the next great age,'" she quoted Cromfield's letter. "Don't try to play the blame game here. I'll win."

Devon glanced at the two of them before his eyes fixed on Molly. "Molls, three to one..."

She threw up her hands. "Fine! We're already probably going to be jobless, homeless, and disowned by the time we get back. What's another trip around the globe?" She grumbled under her breath. "Who wanted the beautiful apartment anyway?

As a child, Rae had always been thrilled with the prospect of flying. It was one of the reasons she'd been so excited to get her friend, Rob's, tatù; his ability to turn into an eagle was like a dream come true. Even when she and Molly had flown to New York on holiday, she'd been secretly over the moon.

Now...she couldn't stand it.

"Hey," Molly said softly, sinking into the chair next to her. "You want some coffee?"

Rae hadn't noticed until this very moment, but she had never before seen her bubbly friends so subdued. "Yeah, hold up your jacket?"

Molly spread her coat like a giant winged shield, and a second later, two steaming espressos were sitting on the corner.

"Milk and eight sugars," Rae grinned weakly. "Just how you like."

Molly took a grateful sip and some of the color returned to her wan cheeks. "So..." she began, hesitant to meet Rae's eyes, "how're you holding up?"

Rae gave a hard laugh. "Oh, let's see... The love of my life doesn't know what to say to me because I finally presented him with the only problem in the world he can't fix. Julian's going to be carrying around a lifetime's worth of so much misplaced guilt that he's probably going to develop a mental disorder. And you? My best friend?" She ticked her fingers as she counted them of. "In the last few months I've gotten you shot at, hit by a car, put on an international psychopath's radar, and have probably traumatized you enough that you'll have to sell your entire shoe collection just to pay for all the therapy."

There was a pause.

"Rae?"

"Yeah?"

"I'd never sell my shoe collection."

Rae grinned in spite of herself and took a long swig of coffee herself. "I don't want it to sound self-martyring or anything, because that's not how I mean it, but sometimes I just wish that I'd never come to Guilder and become friends with you guys. That I'd just done this whole thing alone and kept you all out of it. Somewhere you couldn't get hurt. I can't let that happen."

Molly stared thoughtfully around the terminal, letting the steam from the paper cup warm her face. "You know, when we first started out at Guilder, they offered me the chance to switch roommates."

Rae's head whipped around in surprise. "They did? Who?"

"Carter." Molly took another sip. "The day you arrived. Later that night. He called me into Lanford's office and said that if I'd rather not spend the year living with a Kerrigan, he'd completely understand. I didn't know much about him, except he was the Dean. I didn't know he worked for the Privy Council back then."

Rae's jaw fell open. She'd always thought that Carter hated her when she first started at the school, but that seemed a little extreme. "So what did you say?" she asked curiously.

Molly flashed a grin. "I said I'd take my chances."

Rae shook her head in astonishment, but, when she looked back up, she saw that Molly was staring at her with a very serious expression on her normally-carefree face. Without saying a word, she set down both their coffees and took Rae's hand in her own.

"What I'm trying to tell you is that you're my best friend, Rae. I love you like a sister. These bad things that keep happening to you... None of them are your fault! They're because of the gift you were born with, the same gift I've seen you use to save people's lives a million times. You think you're this dark cloud, bringing misery to everyone around you? You're wrong. You're exactly the opposite. Why do you think you have three people here who would drop everything to go gallivanting around the world with you?"

Rae sucked in a quick breath, a little caught off-balance by the intensity of the question. "I hate to burst your bubble, Molls, but no one ever said the three of you were particularly sane..."

"It's because we love you. We care about you, and we'd do anything for you. But it's a lot more than that." Molly squeezed Rae's hands. "It's because you're doing the right thing. Ever since I've known you, you've always done the right thing. Even when it's breaking all the rules. Even when, technically speaking, it's the wrong thing. Even when it could get you killed. You don't do what's easy—you do what's right. And this, right here, *this* is doing what's right." She broke off with a little shrug, slipping back into classic Molly. "Besides, what else were we supposed to do after graduation?"

Rae looked at her for a minute, sipping her espresso with an oblivious smile, before she jumped on her with a sudden, bone-crushing hug.

Molly giggled and hugged her back, murmuring the occasional, "Don't mess up my hair," before finally pulled away, pushing against Rae's arms. "Rae..." she choked. "Rae!"

Rae loosened her grip at once. "Sorry...too much?"

Molly shook her head, discreetly checking to make sure none of her ribs were broken. "I always forget how over-exuberant you are! You're like a freakin' bodybuilder!"

Rae laughed, feeling for the first time in hours like maybe there was a little light at the end of the tunnel. "Molly?"

"I'm fine." She rolled her shoulders and dropped her head side to side. "I don't think anything's broken."

"No...I mean, good, but..." She bowed her head and spoke to her hands. "Thank you. For saying all that. It really means a lot. I think of you as my sister, too."

Molly beamed back at her, scooting over to make room just as Devon and Julian joined them at their table. "Good," she lowered her voice drastically, "because I'm about to put it to the test."

"Wait..." Rae paused nervously. "What?"

Before she could do anything to stop it, Molly slipped her hand into her long jacket and extracted the cell phone she'd conjured to talk to Cromfield. Her little fingers moved at the speed of light, and the next moment, Rae heard a distant ringing.

Devon heard it at the same time and looked over in surprise. Surprise that quickly turned to scarcely concealed frustration. "Molly—again?! Give it here!"

"Oh, who cares!" Molly fired back. "You already called Carter; they already know where we are. And, no offense, Jules, but Cromfield already knows everything about us so he already knows everything about Luke. I can call him. It won't change a thing."

Devon scowled. "You're just making it so easy for—"

"Tell him, Rae!" Molly insisted, giving her a shameless, pointed stare.

Rae shook her head with a sigh. "Everyone already knows everything, Dev. She's right. All the people we'd be trying to avoid already know where we are. I don't see the harm."

He sighed and held up his hands as the line clicked open. Somewhere, thousands of miles away, Rae heard Luke's groggy voice.

"Hello...?"

"Luke!" Molly squealed, her face lighting up immediately as she pressed the phone to her cheek with a giddy grin. "Oh, I'm so happy you picked up! I just remembered about the time difference." She glanced at her watch with a curious frown. "What's the difference between Osaka and London?"

There was a rustling of sheets. "Wait...Molly?"

Molly rolled her eyes. "Yes, it's your girlfriend. Molly? You remember me? It's only been like...well, actually I'm not sure how long it's actually been—"

"Molly, where the hell are you?! I've been calling you for weeks, but it says your line was disconnected. And now you just call up out of the...wait...did you say Osaka?"

"Yeah, I did, and, to tell you the truth, 'disconnected' was a generous way of putting it. But listen, Luke, the gang and I are flying back to San Francisco in just a couple minutes, and I was wondering if you could do me a really quick favor..." Her sparkling eyes fell on Julian, and Rae looked between them with a small frown.

What the hell did her little friend have up her sleeve now?

Chapter 10

"I just don't get it! I've no earthly idea why you would think it was a good move to involve the San Francisco police force," Devon said for the millionth time.

He and Molly had been going at it during almost the entire flight from Japan, and Rae was just about at her wit's end. She loved them both dearly, but it seemed like when their stress level passed a certain threshold, they started bickering back and forth like siblings. On the one hand, she thought it was kind of adorable, the brother-sister relationship they'd so clearly established back at school, and of course she was thrilled that her best friend and her boyfriend loved each other enough to fight like family. On the other hand—it was driving her nuts!

"I'm about to shock the both of you," Rae muttered, lifting her fingers. "That's right, ladies and gentlemen, fasten your seatbelts. Shocking in three...two..."

They paused long enough in their diatribe to shoot her a bitter look. Both were rather insulted she hadn't taken their side, and when she'd said that they were both 'big kids who could make their own decisions,' they'd rightly taken that as more than a little condescending.

"Don't be silly, Rae," Molly sniffed. "You know you can't play around with electricity on a plane. We could all go down screaming."

"It might be a great new way for me to test my 'I can't die' theory," Rae said sarcastically.

Devon pointedly ignored this and turned again to Molly with a crooked grin. "Actually, that would be great. See, that way we could meet even *more* of the California police force."

"We're not joining the force, Devon Wardell," she shot back, pulling herself up to her full, if rather lacking, height. "We are simply accepting a favor from my awesome boyfriend. And, to be perfectly honest, a little thank-you might be in order."

Devon raised his eyebrows, pulling himself up to *his* full height, which, in all fairness and handsome beauty, was much more impressive than Molly's. "Let's just see how badly this blows up in our faces, alright? Then we'll see who's going to be going around handing out thank-yous."

Rae rolled her eyes and stuffed pillow over her face, wishing like hell she hadn't helped Molly call Luke right before take-off. The premise had been good. Luke's cousin worked for the police academy in San Francisco.

While Luke's cousin didn't have any information yet about what had gone on in the penthouse, or at least any information that he was able to share, he did say that he could let them go in and examine the 'crime scene' without a whole lot of red tape, by putting them on the list as 'friends and/or family.' While Molly had enthusiastically thanked him for the help, Devon had brought to mind the obvious problem that Benjamin Mills could simply take one look at them and have security throw them out of the building. *Again.*

As the sound of their bickering faded to a merciful background hum, Rae turned her eyes instead to Julian. While he'd accepted Devon and Rae's no-blame censure back in Osaka, Rae got the feeling that his mind hadn't changed in the least. He still felt one hundred percent responsible for whatever ended up happening to Benjamin Mills, and, to be honest, Rae couldn't blame him. Not that it *was* his fault; it absolutely wasn't, but Cromfield had planted the idea in his head like a little seed. He'd made Julian into the one who'd single-handedly rushed them out of San Francisco, away from the hybrid who'd ended up needing their help the most.

But even more than that, Cromfield had completely undermined Julian's confidence by hitting him at his very core—his tatù. He'd taken something as fundamental as it got and warped it so *who Julian was*, a psychic, his very essence, was distorted. He'd lost his grip on reality, unable to tell if what he was thinking was real or something created by a lunatic madman. He couldn't trust his thoughts; he couldn't trust his visions; he couldn't trust himself. And now here he was on the plane, visibly losing himself in the aftermath.

"Julian—hey," she whispered, peering across the aisle.

He was leaning back in his chair with his eyes closed, but she didn't think he was sleeping. She thought he was probably just avoiding the Molly vs. Devon blowout like she was. Sure enough, he opened his dark eyes and gazed out at her across the dim interior.

"How...are you doing?" she asked, repeating Molly's over-simplified question from before.

The corners of his mouth twitched, though his eyes were hard. "Great. You?"

She grinned. "Peachy. Hey, listen," she leaned further across the aisle, "no matter what we see over there, no matter what's happened, you have to know that it's—"

"We're landing, Rae," he interrupted softly.

She stopped short. "What?"

"That's San Francisco." He cocked his head towards the window, and began gathering up his things like the rest of the passengers. "We're here."

Well, saved by the freaking bell.

Rae eyed him suspiciously, but let it go. She didn't like the look that had settled on his lovely face; it was disturbingly free of all emotion. There was no blame, there was no fight, there wasn't even any anger. It was just...blank. And unsettlingly decided. On what? Rae didn't know.

With extreme reluctance, she tuned back in to the conversation at hand.

"So get a freaking scooter then," Devon was saying in hushed exasperation. "I don't know why you feel the need to run that by me. And I certainly don't see how it's relevant to the situation at hand—"

"Guys!" Rae put a hand on each of their knees. "We're landing."

"Oh..." Molly glanced out the window. "Already? I feel like we just took off..."

Rae closed her eyes with a grimace. *She was going to kill them both.*

It was a bitter cold night in San Francisco. Despite the balmy summer afternoons, the salty ocean breeze chilled the evening hours, and the second they stepped into the terminal, Rae ducked into the nearest bathroom to conjure them all some warmer clothes.

Remind me to thank Ethan when we get home, she thought, distributing them to her friends in silence. *This one has saved our necks quite a few times now...*

They moved through customs without a hitch, and were just heading outside towards the cabs when a familiar face came sprinting into view.

Rae stepped back in astonishment as Luke blurred past her and scooped Molly up in a huge hug.

Molly, who had unfortunately been turned the other way, screamed, "Attacker! Attacker!" before turning around and seeing her beloved boyfriend grinning ear to ear.

"Luke!" she squealed in shock. "What the hell are you doing here?!"

He kissed her firmly on the mouth before setting her back on her toes. "You finally check in after almost a month to let me know where you are and you expect me to let you slip away again? I don't think so, Skye." Still clutching her tightly to his side, he turned around and greeted the others for the first time. "Hey, guys, long time no see!"

Rae's mouth fell open in a huge smile and she ran over to hug him as well, but Devon and Julian shared a brief, troubled look. After Rae stepped back, Devon went forward to shake Luke's hand in greeting, but, as he did, he couldn't help but ask, "Hey, man, it's good to see you. But, uh...this isn't, like, a Xavier Knights' sanctioned meet and greet or anything—"

"No, no, no," Luke assured him quickly. "I came on my own. I was a little, uh," he searched for the right word with a faint grin, "*upset* to be left behind. But Miss Skye over here assured me that it was all for the best."

"It was!" She stood up on her tiptoes to kiss him again. "It was way too dangerous, babe. I actually got hit by a car by this crazy girl at a Texas rodeo. Then there was this rogue donkey that chased after us in Peru. Of course, that one wasn't really supernatural, but it was just as scary—"

"Molly," Julian pressed, tapping his wrist, "Benjamin Mills?"

Luke frowned slightly at his tone, and looked the four friends up and down for the first time.

Rae didn't need to have super-powers to read the slight widening in his eyes as they swept over her and the others. Between the tired eyes, the worn faces, and the not-quite-fitting hastily- conjured clothes, they must have looked a little worse for wear.

"He's right," she said quickly. "We've got to get to the penthouse as soon as possible."

"Actually..." Luke said with a bit of hesitation. "That's not going to exactly be possible for at least another few hours. You see, they're still investigating the crime scene, and, until the section chief says it's clear, there's no getting in or out."

"Are you bloody kidding me?!" Julian exclaimed, throwing up his hands. The blank façade had finally cracked. The forced hollow indifference had given way to all the feelings he'd been keeping locked inside. "Is the guy dead?" He stared Luke right in the eyes as he pressed him to answer the question. "Just tell me that. Is Benjamin Mills dead?"

"I..." Luke glanced at Rae in bewilderment. "I don't know, Julian." His brow creased in frustration. "Molly said you all just met the guy. Not to sound really insensitive, but why do you care so much—"

Julian's eyes flashed. "Because if he's dead, I'm the one who killed him. And *don't* tell me that's not the case, Kerrigan," he snapped at Rae before she could disagree. "I don't need to have your fancy fox ink to hear what Cromfield said to you on the phone. Seems I've been an invaluable help. He couldn't have gotten to Mills without me."

Rae's heart sank as she understood. So he'd actually heard Cromfield himself. That's why he was inconsolable.

Luke stared on in silence as Julian stormed off to the cabs. The other three stood in charged silence. His eyes traced back and forth between them before finally landing on Molly.

"What the hell happened to you guys out there?"

At a loss, Molly turned to Rae, who hung her head with a sigh. "It's a really long story..."

Much to everyone's chagrin, the five of them were forced to stay the night at a nearby hotel until the penthouse would be officially open for viewing in the morning. With nerves already stretched past the breaking point, Julian protested it every step of the way.

"Just turn us invisible, and we can all go inside," he insisted, bouncing impatiently from foot to foot in the hotel lobby as Molly booked them some rooms.

"Invisible?" Luke had repeated in astonishment. "Rae, you can do—"

"I'll put on my glasses and pretend to be a blind forensic psychic, and you can turn into a wolf and pretend to be my Seeing-Eye dog. I don't really care. Let's just go!"

Rae pursed her lips as she considered that one. "You want me to pretend to be your...your Seeing- Eye dog? That's where we're at?"

Julian threw up his hands and smacked Devon in the chest to stop his laughter. "I don't know, I'm just trying to think of a way to get us in—"

"Hang on," Luke cut him off as he pulled out his buzzing phone. "It's my cousin." He answered it and walked a few paces away, pretending to ignore Julian's following him. "Hey, thanks for getting back to me so quick. Do you have any kind of update on Benjamin Mills?"

His face creased in a thoughtful frown, and Rae thought that Julian might honestly be on the verge of a heart attack. She walked over quietly and slipped her hand in his, relieved when he didn't flinch away, gathering her up in his arms instead.

"I don't know what I'll do," he whispered.

She looked up to see his eyes full of tears.

"I don't know what I'll do if he's dead. I should have known— I should have known it wasn't real."

Rae patted the back of his hair, staring at Luke over his shoulder and trying to decipher his expression. The connection was so bad, that even using Devon's tatù, she was having a hard time hearing anything that was said. Luke nodded a few times, his face still scrunched up in concern, before he thanked his cousin and headed over.

"Well?" Rae prompted, every muscle in her body tensed to explode.

Luke glanced at Julian with a small smile. "He's alive."

There was a small explosion as Julian sank down onto the floor, inadvertently dragging Rae down with him. "*Oh, thank bloody goodness...*" he kept saying over and over, burying his face in his hands. When he finally looked up, his face was lit with his first genuine smile in what felt like years. He laughed aloud at Rae's disheveled expression and lifted her gently to her feet.

"Thank you," he said to Luke, shaking his hand before pulling him in for a brief, one-armed hug. "Really, you have no idea how much. *Thank you*." He ran his hands back over his face, grinning uncontrollably as Devon walked forward with a huge, beaming smile and clapped his shoulder.

"I wasn't worried for a second," Devon lied casually. "Not one second."

"Yeah," Luke chuckled, "right."

"Oh, me neither," Julian teased back, still clutching his chest in utter relief.

Rae giggled aloud. "Yep—it's every day that you ask me to become a Seeing-Eye dog to help you sneak into a crime scene..."

Julian looked at her excitedly. "You know, I still think that could have worked..."

At that moment, Molly returned with a handful of keys. "So, I was only able to get three rooms because it was pretty short notice, but then I thought, that's perfect!" She gestured to herself and Luke, followed by Rae and Devon, and then Julian. "Sorry, Jules. You know, maybe you should text that girl, Angel, again. Rae told me she was really beautiful."

Julian shot Rae and accusatory look, and she grinned innocently. "What? She is! I saw it for myself!"

He ruffled her hair and snatched away his key with a grin. "You know, maybe I will. But just for future reference, let's stay out of my personal thoughts, okay?"

Rae pretended to pout. "If you want me to..."

She and Devon quickly bid the others goodnight and headed upstairs to their room. Rae had been bouncing back and forth from one end of the globe to another so frequently that she no longer had any real concept of day and night. She slept when she was tired. She woke when she wasn't. And right now, while Devon in his usual freakish manner decided to put in a few hours at the gym, she wanted to take a bath.

The room Molly had booked was almost as big as the bedroom in Heath Hall, and the bathtub was a thing of wonder. Rae stared in gleeful anticipation at the little jets coming out the side as she held out her hand and conjured a bottle of vanilla-scented bubble bath.

"Just what the doctor ordered..." she said aloud as the room filled up with clouds of steam.

When the tub was finally full to the brim and topped with an almost impenetrable layer of bubbles, she dropped her fluffy hotel robe and stepped in. Her eyes closed automatically as every muscle in her aching body cried out in relief. She hadn't realized how wound up she was until she finally laid down on something that wasn't either a motel cot in Uganda or an airplane seat. The warm water slowly eased her knotted muscles loose, and she laid back her head against the side of the tub with a little moan of contentment.

Benjamin Mills was alive. Julian was smiling again. They were heading home to London. And, together, with a little adult supervision, they would figure out what to do about Cromfield.

Everything was slowly piecing itself back together...

"Well, someone went a little crazy with the bubbles."

With a startled shriek, Rae slipped underwater, inhaling a mouthful of suds before resurfacing with a gasp. She wiped the soapy water from her eyes and looked up to see Devon grinning at her from the doorway, still in his newly conjured work-out clothes.

"Did you," she spat out a bubble, "did you finish already?"

"No," he chuckled, "I lied down on the chair to do some weights and then woke up five minutes later to see that I'd fallen asleep. I thought I might take it easy today."

She nodded seriously, smoothing back her soaking curls and trying to look less like what she feared resembled a drowned mouse. "That was my plan, too."

"I can see that," he said, taking a seat on the edge of the bathtub. Even though it was impossible for him to see anything under the thick curtain of snowy bubbles, Rae blushed. "You know, I didn't really peg you for a bubble-bath kind of girl."

She grinned. "There's a lot you still don't know about me, Wardell."

"Is that right?"

"But, no, I'm not usually the bath type. I was just *trying* to relax, when someone walked in and scared me half to death."

His brow creased in adorable mock concern. "And now you're all wound up again?"

She sniffed self-righteously. "That's right."

"Well, maybe I can help you out with that..."

Without another word, he walked around to the side of the tub and got down on his knees behind Rae. She tried turning, a little self-conscious as to what he might be doing, but his hands slipped down over her shoulders as he began gently rubbing her back.

"That feels incredible," she moaned, tilting her head forward as his fingers wound up into her hair. "Where did you learn to do this so well?"

"Oh, you know," he teased, "I've practiced on *lots* of women..."

She splashed a handful of bubbles behind her and he laughed. "Lots of women, huh?"

"Oh, yes," his lips grazed the back of her neck and she shivered, "thousands."

The two of them lapsed into smiling silence as he pushed her gently forward and began working out the stress in the rest of her back. She couldn't help but grin as his hands dipped lower and lower, gently caressing her skin with strong, but delicate, hands. When she finally sat back up, there was a cloud of bubbles on the tip of her nose. She turned around with a grin and he laughed, nuzzling his nose against hers to take some for himself.

"Let's see the beard," he challenged.

She dipped her chin forward and came up with something fit to rival St. Nick. "How's that?"

He frowned critically. "It's not bad, not bad. But I think that I can do better, Kerrigan."

"Oh, really?"

"You'll see..."

She burst out in peals of laughter as he began to climb, fully-clothed, into the tub. The water immediately soaked through his dark jeans and tee-shirt, but he pretended not to notice. Luckily, the space was big enough, and he settled in on the opposite side so they were looking at each other, their knees touching in the middle.

"Let's see then," she said once she finally got a hold of herself.

With the expression of an Olympic diver, he lowered his face to the bubbles, turning this way and that, before pulling up with a magnificent snowy beard. Rae applauded politely, wriggling around as his hands pulled her ankles closer under the water and began tickling her toes.

"You know," she giggled, "I could maybe get used to you with a beard."

His eyebrows shot up with a smile. "Oh, yeah?"

"Yep. It's...pretty sexy, actually. A goatee kind of beard, all smooth and sexy and even across you face. Very hot."

He shot her a wink as his hand travelled further up her leg. "I'd make sure to dye it white."

There was a bit more underwater adjusting as he reached forward and pulled her to his side of the tub, turning her around so she could lean back on his chest comfortably.

"What a day..." he mused, gazing up at the ceiling.

She sighed and pulled his arms tighter around her. "We're having too many of those."

He leaned his head down to kiss the base of her neck. "This is almost done. We'll be back in London soon. And if we can survive whatever round of Spanish Inquisition-style punishments Carter has in mind, we're going to be fine."

"But what's going to have changed?" she asked wearily. "We still have half a list to go and Julian can't—"

"What's going to change is that we already did the first half. We have a whole list of people who can back up what we're saying, and, tell you the truth, all I really think we'll need is Mills. This had to have given him a scare. We'll have him come back with us to London to give a full report."

Rae paused, thinking this over. "You really think the PC will believe us?"

"We'll *make* them believe us."

She shook her head doubtfully, and he tilted back her head.

"Hey," he said, kissing the tip of her nose, "you are the most beautiful, amazing, reckless, talented girl I've ever met. If anyone can make them believe us, it's you."

She felt a warm blush blossom in her cheeks and she looked back down at the bubbles with a grin. "You're just saying that so I'll conjure you dry clothes."

He chuckled, hands reaching down to tickle her sides. "Yeah, dry clothes would be nice..."

"Stop!" she shrieked, splashing water out of the tub as she writhed around, laughing. "Stop or I won't do it!"

"Rae," he shook his head, "don't be silly. I'm never going to stop. And you don't have to do it. I'm perfectly content to walk down to Mills' place without clothes."

"Without clothes?" she panted, trying to catch her breath, a mischievous grin on her face. "I can't even imagine it."

He gave her a look of false concern, lifting his shirt off above his head. "You can't? How careless of me."

"Yes," she sniffed, eyes wandering down his bare chest as he reached for the buckle on his pants, "it is rather careless."

"Well," his eyes sparkled with a grin, "let me help you remember..."

Rae woke up the next morning feeling alive and refreshed for
what felt like the first time in a very long time. She lay in bed,
running her fingers through Devon's bed-tousled hair until he
opened his eyes, and smiled.

"Good morning," she said warmly.

He stretched with a huge yawn. "Good morning."

"We said we'd meet the others downstairs at eight, and it's
seven-forty-five. We should get up and get dressed."

"Yeah, or we could hop in the bath again." He grinned, rolling
on top of her and showering her with kisses.

She giggled, hiding under her hands. "As much as I'd love to
do that, we have a hospital to get to, a mystery to solve, and a
flight back to London so we can get tarred and feathered."

He yawned again. "Just your average Wednesday."

"It's Sunday."

"Close enough."

They met the others down in the lobby, and were pleased to
find that everyone looked as bright and refreshed as they did.
Molly and Luke couldn't keep their hands off each other, and
even Julian had recovered that long-lost spring in his step.

"So," Molly grinned smugly, "what did you guys do last
night?"

Rae and Devon shared a glance before he said, "Nothing
much, just went to the gym."

"Yeah," Rae added casually. "I took a bath."

Molly looked momentarily disappointed before her face lit up
once more. "Oh. Well, that sounds nothing at all like our night,
does it, babe?"

Luke blushed but chuckled. "Remember that little talk we
had, something about we never kiss and tell?"

Molly flipped back her hair. "No. I must have been distracted." Her eyes swept to Julian with a kind of gloating pity. "Sorry, Jules, guess you must have gone straight to bed."

His eyes sparkled. "Actually, I was up for a while. I decided to give Angel a call, like you suggested. Things are...good."

"Really?" She clapped her hands together, bouncing on her toes. "Jules, that's so great!"

"Who's Angel?" Luke asked curiously.

Molly gushed. "Just this blonde bombshell Julian was dating, and now it looks like he is again. She has this awesome tatù where she can, like, stun-freeze people in place."

Luke chuckled. "Another couple who both have ink? Geez— do you guys ever follow your own rules?"

Rae shrugged, shooting Devon a grin. "We've set a bad example..."

"It's a terrible precedent," he agreed, shaking his head with a smile.

Molly ignored this, lowering her voice to a dramatic whisper. "Julian and she use the freeze tatù thing during sex."

"Molly!" Rae exclaimed, shooting her friend a chiding look as Julian blushed to the heavens.

"How the hell do you even know that?" he asked incredulously. He shot a sudden mortified look at Rae, who threw up her hands in the air.

"No! Gross! I know what you're thinking, but I didn't see a thing when I was inside your head. And by the way...again...gross."

Molly shrugged unabashedly. "You kind of implied it once in an unguarded moment, and I read between the lines. It's nothing to be ashamed of, Jules. It's actually kind of hot."

He shook his head with a long-suffering sigh. "How is it that you remember every single detail about my personal life, but when I ask you something basic, like, did you remember to get our parking validated, you look at me like I'm speaking Swedish?"

"Julian," Molly said with gentle patience, "I think the real question is why you keep giving me the tickets to get validated."

"You know," Luke threw his arm around her shoulders as the five of them headed out the door, "sometimes I'm really glad I never went to school with you guys."

Chapter 11

The five of them had made if halfway to San Francisco Memorial Hospital before Luke got a call, saying Mills had been released that morning and was already back at home. After handing the irritated cab driver a generous tip, they turned around and doubled back the way they had come.

Rae had only been to San Francisco as a child, when she accompanied Uncle Argyle on a business trip, and she found the hilly roads and constant up and down movement almost nauseating. "I miss Guilder," she leaned over and whispered into Molly's ear.

Molly shook back her crimson hair and patted her friend's knee. "I do, too. I feel like, maybe, if we'd stopped for a traditional fish and chips somewhere between the Azores and St. Petersburg, we could have wrapped this thing up already."

Rae glanced around the strange streets with a grin, feeling exactly the same way. They were on unfamiliar ground here. Shoot, they *had* been for a long time. It was going to feel good to get home. "Well, I can always conjure us up some fish and chips," she offered graciously.

Molly made a horrified face, probably remembering the cookie Rae had tried to conjure in Texas, before quickly catching herself with a casual smile. "Oh...that's okay. You, um, save your strength. We don't know what Mills is going to tell us when we get there. Best to do it on an empty stomach."

As if on cue, the cab suddenly cut across three lanes of traffic and rolled to a stop along the curb. They thanked the driver profusely and piled out onto the sidewalk, staring up at the tall building, with rather anxious expressions. It was so strange to think that Cromfield had been here just two days before. He'd actually been standing in this exact same spot.

Rae shuddered and Devon's hand automatically found hers. Their eyes met, and in his she found nothing but calm reassurance. Without saying a word, she nodded her head, and the five of them headed inside.

If Mill's trigger-happy security team recognized them from before, they certainly didn't let on now. They were distracted and demoralized, having let their building's prize customer be taken down by some middle-aged man.

Middle-aged, Rae thought with a derisive snort. *Middle Ages is more like it.*

They piled into the elevator and headed to the top floor, each one looking a bit nervous as to what exactly they were going to find. The obvious questions weighed heavy on them all.

Why had Cromfield left this man alive when he'd killed all the others? What the hell was so special about Benjamin Mills? And, then, of course, there was always the good old standard: Was this some kind of terrible trap?

As usual, Devon seemed to be thinking along the same lines as Rae. Without saying a word, he reached out and pressed the 'stop' button to pause their climb.

"Listen," he said quickly, "I think we should maybe have some kind of strategy for when we go in there. Cromfield talked to Rae on the phone about Mills himself. There's a good chance he guessed that she'd be coming back here to check in on him. This could be a set-up."

"Or he could have just seen it in my thoughts," Julian muttered.

Devon looked up at him sharply. "Did he?"

Julian paused uncertainly, but Devon didn't give an inch of ground.

"You felt it all the other times he did. I mean, you *really* felt it. That hasn't happened again, has it?"

"No," Julian admitted. "I've been trying to keep him out, but so far it's been really easy; so, realistically, he probably hasn't even tried yet."

"Good." Rae took over, saying a silent prayer of thanks that Cromfield's 'inside guy' approach was at least temporarily out of service. "So here's the plan. I go in first—"

"Absolutely not!" Devon and Julian and Luke all cut her off at the same time.

She looked up at their stern faces in surprise before turning to Molly, who simply shrugged obliviously. "I thought it was a good start. You can't die."

"What?" Luke murmured, but one look from Molly shushed him.

"Thank you," Rae said gratefully before turning to the guys. "Alrightie. Think about it, boys. This is no time to play 'who's got the bigger tatù.' Hate to break it to you, but I do. By a long shot. I'm going in first."

"Yeah, you're also the one who this whack-job wants to turn into some kind of child bride," Luke countered. "You should be the last one in. Or, better yet, you should stay invisible."

Devon actually turned to him with great appreciation before saying, "My thoughts exactly."

Rae cocked her head impatiently. "Do I have to light myself on fire again? Prove my worth or something? We have no idea how he's been subduing all these hybrids. There could be some serious firepower on the other side of that door."

"All the more reason for you to stay behind."

"All the more reason for her to go in first," Molly piped up. The boys glared down at her, but she held her ground. "I'm sorry, but it just makes sense. We didn't make it this far by keeping Rae on the sidelines; we're not going to start now. If it makes anybody feel any better, she and I can go in together. She'll be invisible out in front, and I'll provide cover fire."

Rae's heart warmed with gratitude as she and Molly shared a quick smile. Her best friend might be an over-talkative shopaholic, but, on days like today, there was no one she'd rather have by her side.

The 'Devon and Julian' super-hero team might be legendary around school and with the Privy Council, but it was time for the boys to step aside. There was a new dynamic duo on the rise.

If it was possible, this plan seemed to make the fellas even more upset, but Rae and Molly ignored their protests completely, pulling out the 'stop' as they flew once more to the top.

The second the doors opened, Rae vanished from sight. Molly kept one extended hand discreetly on the back of her coat to keep track of where she was, and then the two of them launched themselves into the apartment.

Rae had expected an army, a battalion, for Cromfield to slowly spin around on a leather recliner, wearing a monocle, with a white cat perched on his lap.

Instead, a rather confused-looking Benjamin Mills stumbled in from the kitchen.

"Oh, hey, Molly," he said, rubbing his head but walking forward with an eager smile. "Did you finally agree to take me up on that coffee date?"

Molly's cheeks flamed an incriminating red as the boys poured out of the elevator. Luke, in particular, looked rather aggressive as he strode forward and placed his arm firmly around Molly's tiny waist.

Benjamin studied them for a moment, before pursing his lips. "So...that whole flirting act? Just a sad attempt to get inside my apartment, was it?"

"Sorry," Molly cringed, "but it was for your own safety."

He laughed, waving his hand dismissively. "It's okay; I kinda figured. It seemed a little too good to be true."

The whole time they'd been talking, Rae had been studying Benjamin, with a critical eye to rival that of Madame Elpis. He didn't look hurt, he didn't look traumatized. In fact, other than being a bit unsteady on his feet, he looked perfectly normal.

"So what the hell happened to you?" Rae asked pointedly, reappearing into view.

Benjamin fell back with a cry, clutching his chest as she appeared, sitting on his sofa. "How did you just...? You can disa...? How long have you been here?!"

"Oh, relax," she said dismissively, "I just came in with Molly a second ago."

"Why, Benjamin?" Devon was watching him with eyes just as intent as Rae's. "Doing something you weren't exactly proud of?"

Julian stepped forward, finishing his thoughts. "Something you'd maybe rather hide?"

Rae glanced confusedly between them, before, all at once, it clicked. Of course! They had to consider the possibility that whatever Cromfield was up to, Benjamin could be in on it; the only hybrid in hundreds of years not to be murdered by the man. There had to be more to that story than met the eye.

Benjamin threw up his hands. "Hey! I know what you're thinking. You said this guy was a real monster, right? That he was some kind of killer?" He shook his head innocently. "But I'm telling you guys, except for kind of drugging me at the end of the evening, he was a perfect gentleman."

As Rae watched him, wondering what to believe, a sudden tentative buzzing floated up to the edges of her skin. Curious, she momentarily relaxed and let her body choose whatever tatù it was wanting. Much to her surprise, it was Ellie's. She considered this with a small frown. Ellie was gifted with both knowledge and understanding. That meant that she not only had the greatest photographic memory in the history of the world, but she also knew the intentions behind everything she learned. She understood its truth or sincerity. That being said, Rae had only seen it applied to written texts. It wasn't like Ellie was a human polygraph machine. But who knew; maybe there was more to the ink than met the eye.

With a little frown, she crossed the room to where Benjamin stood, pushing him firmly down on the couch. Then, keeping him fixed in her gaze, she sat down on the accompanying chair and took his hand, hoping the shared physical connection would help her make sense of what was going on.

"Uh, Rae," Devon ventured tentatively behind Benjamin. "Whatchya doing?"

Benjamin looked just as confused to be holding her hand. "Yeah, um, no offense, I'm really flattered, but that flirting trick won't really work on me twice. I know what you girls are—"

"Would you shut up?" Rae growled between her teeth, focusing all her concentration on the tatù. "Now tell me what's going on. And don't you lie to me, Benjamin." She squeezed his fingers in a warning. "I'll know."

Benjamin gulped. "Little tight there." When she released the hold a fraction, he nodded. "Okay, okay. The day after you guys left, I got a call from my office that we had a potential investor who wanted to meet with me. Now, let me preface this with the fact that that isn't unusual, okay? We get generous donors all the time, and, as CEO, it's my job to schmooze them."

Devon rolled his eyes. "Yeah, yeah, we get it. You weren't incredibly *stupid* for letting some stranger up into your apartment after we told you someone was coming here to kill you. Go on."

Benjamin flushed. "Yeah, well, when you put it like that..."

"Get to it already, Benjamin," Molly commanded, little sparks flying from her fingers.

He shook his head at all of them and sighed. "Well, we went out to dinner, and I told him about my plans for the upcoming quarter. He seemed really," he glanced around nervously, "well, to be honest, he seemed really nice. He was asking all the right questions, really engaged in what we were talking about. When I mentioned that I had several prototype designs back at my apartment, and he asked if he could see them, I didn't think it was a big deal. Because *I* asked *him*, you know? So why would I have thought that—"

"Why would you have thought literally inviting a stranger up to your apartment after we told you someone was trying to kill you was an incredibly *stupid* idea?" Julian rolled his eyes. "Not a clue."

"Yes, well, I maintain it could have happened to anyone—"

A bolt of lightning shattered a nearby vase. "*Benjamin*!"

"Sorry, right. Anyway, we headed back here, and I showed him everything I'd been working on. He took a phone call, and then we continued chatting about one of the prototypes. He seemed really interested in investing, so I went to pour us some drinks. That's when everything...gets a little blurry."

The whole time Benjamin had been talking, Rae had been holding onto his hand, letting the unique tatù work its magic as she centered her brain, and concentrated more than she ever had in her life. She didn't think he was lying. As stupid as this genius might be, she actually thought he was telling the truth.

"He slipped something into your drink," Molly summarized, her voice softening for the first time as she looked at Benjamin in pity.

Benjamin hung his head. "Yeah. He actually seemed really excited about it. Said that I was one of the first to try his new concoction."

"New concoction?" Devon asked shrewdly. "What does that mean?"

Benjamin shrugged. "I don't know. The doctors at the hospital didn't know what it was either. They said most date-rape-type drugs make you black out and you lose your memory. This wasn't anything like that. I was still aware of everything going on around me, I remember it all perfectly, I just...couldn't move. Couldn't even think to move."

At these words, Julian fell back a step, his bright face suddenly darkening as he looked at Benjamin with something close to dread.

Rae noticed it as well, but made Benjamin keep talking. "What happened next?" she murmured.

"He took a blood and hair sample before propping me up with a pillow and going on his way. The whole time he was really nice about it, even apologizing while he had to pin-prick me. He and the girl both were quite nice."

"The girl?" Devon asked sharply, taking a step forward. "What girl?"

"Jennifer?" Rae didn't need to use Carter's tatù to know what girl.

Apparently neither did Julian. His voice dropped down to a low whisper, rough with a million things that would forever go unsaid. "You're wrong. It's not Jennifer. It's Angel."

"Wait..." Luke struggled to catch up with the others as they hurried after Julian down the street. "I don't understand. Angel, like Julian's girlfriend, Angel?"

"She's not my girlfriend," Julian shot back, barely slowing down as he crossed the street. A taxi honked its horn as it screeched to a stop, but he just slapped the hood and kept walking.

"Jules," Devon jogged to his side, "slow down for a second. Let's just think."

Julian stopped as quickly as he'd taken off, causing a sea of bewildered pedestrians to part suddenly around him. "What's there to think about? I think it's pretty clear what happened."

Molly, Rae, and Luke caught up with them the next minute.

"It's not clear to me..." Luke said.

Before anyone could say anything, Rae sighed and pushed them all into the little diner they'd inadvertently stopped in front of. She flashed five fingers to the waitress before grabbing a stack of menus for the table and ushering them all to the back. This was going to be a bad talk. One with no good solution. They weren't going to do it out on a public street. And they weren't going to do it running on fumes.

"Rae, what the hell are we doing here?" Devon murmured as she manhandled them all down into the farthest booth.

"What?" she whispered back. "You want to have this out in front of half of San Francisco?"

His mouth hardened into a grim line. "That's a good point."

Without further discussion, they settled down in a charged silence as Rae called for five coffees. The waitress set them down and pulled out her pad to take an order, but Molly discreetly shook her head and the woman hurried on her way. Once it was clear that they were alone, Rae cast a quick glance at Julian.

His face was a hard mask, unlike anything she'd ever seen before. Out of the four of them, Julian was undoubtedly the most soft-spoken; the one who, despite his jaw-dropping looks, was remarkably shy when it came to female attention and the idea of relationships. He'd taken a chance on Angel, that much was clear, and Rae couldn't imagine a worse way for it to have played out.

"How..." she almost fell silent at the look on his face, but gritted her teeth and forced herself to keep going, "How did you meet her?"

He pursed his lips, looking down at the table, his eyes burning a hole through the varnished wood.

Devon cast him a look of the utmost sympathy, and then gently got the ball rolling. "It was in Italy, right?" Julian kept silent and he gave him a little nudge. "Jules, in Italy?"

With an almost inaudible sigh, Julian raised his eyes to the opposite wall. There was a strange, lifeless look in them; that same deadening Rae had seen getting started on the plane. "Florence," he finally answered. "We met in Florence."

Rae nodded and resisted the strong urge to give him a hug. "And...who met whom?"

"She met me." His lips turned up in a hard smile that didn't reach his eyes, "but she would have, wouldn't she?"

On the other end of the table, Luke cast a hesitant glance around. "I'm sorry, guys, I know I'm a little behind, but I still have no idea what you're—"

"Angel was never really my girlfriend," Julian explained sharply. "Apparently, she was working with Cromfield the whole time."

Molly bit her lip, her eyes brimming with little tears. "Oh, Jules... But, are you sure? It could have been any girl Benjamin was talking about. Rae mentioned Jennifer. She's a die-hard Cromfield fan. Rae, you should have used Carter's—"

"I'm sure," Julian's voice barely cut above the din of the diner. "The second he started talking about that mystery drug they slipped him. It was how he said it. Not that he couldn't move, but that he 'couldn't *think* to move.' That's how Angel's ink works. It gets inside your head, so it doesn't really matter how strong you are. Your own mind holds you hostage."

"But hasn't this been going on for hundreds of years?" Luke asked quietly. "She's not immortal. She couldn't have—"

"Her father had it, and his father, and his father." Julian shook his head. "Cromfield's probably just been collecting them, generation after generation, to help him with his...work."

Devon leaned forward and clapped a protective hand on his best friend's shoulder. "When you called her last night, did she—"

Julian's face fell into his hands with a miserable sigh. "I didn't call her last night. I saw her."

Rae shot Devon a quick look. "You saw her?" she repeated. "As in...at the hotel?"

This girl had been right under their noses? Just two doors down?

His face tightened and he nodded. "When I called, she said she was in town." He shook his head with a wry grin. "Of course she was, right? She was here for Benjamin."

"Jules," Molly put her hand over his, "you couldn't have known."

His head jerked up and he pulled away. "But that's just our running line now, isn't it? That I 'couldn't have known.' Couldn't have known about Japan. Couldn't have known about Angel..." He looked up at Rae without seeming to think about it, his eyes a million miles away as he remembered. "She was so interested in every part of my life," he said softly. "My school, my job, my friends. It's how Cromfield got into my head. You can't do that with someone you don't know. You can watch them, sure, but you can't get inside their head like that. But I...I trusted her. I told her whatever she wanted to know. And she used it to offer me up to him. Now everything I do, everything I think...I can't trust any of it." He pushed suddenly to his feet. "And you guys shouldn't either."

Without another word, he started heading to the door, leaving his friends in a shocked circle behind him. Unfortunately for him, two of those friends were gifted with super-speed. Before he could make it past the fourth table, Devon and Rae were in front of him, pushing him to a stop.

"You are *not* just going to take off on us," Rae said firmly. "Under no circumstances."

Devon's eyes shone with concern. "Jules, I can't imagine how you must be feeling right now, but Rae's right. You going off on your own doesn't help anybody. In fact, it puts us all at even more risk. You've got to stay."

Julian stared between them and it looked like it was taking every bit of self-control he had just to keep himself together. "It's not safe when I'm here. Cromfield hasn't tried to get back into my head yet, but what about when he does? I can't stop him; I'm not strong enough. And whatever we're planning when he does, whatever course of action we've decided...he'll know."

"We'll cross that bridge when we come to it," Rae said, with a lot more certainty than she actually felt. "We're not splitting up. No matter what. End of story."

"Rae, think," he pressed quietly. "He's essentially made me his inside man. I don't know how to stop that. And I'll be damned if anyone else gets hurt because of my mistakes—"

"Julian, they weren't mistakes," Devon interrupted heatedly. "You were targeted. Cromfield saw you were one of Rae's best friends and a member of the Privy Council. Not to mention, you have the same bloody tatù! This had nothing to do with what you may or may not have decided; you were marked from the start."

"He's right," Rae added fiercely. The look on Julian's face was breaking her heart; she'd do anything to make it go away. "If you didn't fall for Angel, they would have sent someone else, then someone else. Maybe even gone after your family. You didn't have a choice, Julian. It's not some tagline. It's the truth."

He threw up his hands. "It doesn't matter! What's done is done! He's in my head now; it's over!"

Devon continued to argue, but Rae had gone suddenly quiet. There was an advantage here; they'd just been too overwhelmed to see it.

As the boys went back and forth, a little smile crept up her face as a plan started slowly forming. "It's not over," she said softly. "Not by a long-shot."

Her sudden change of tone made Devon pause, and he looked down at her curiously. Even Julian turned, wondering what was going on inside her head.

"You see, Cromfield may have temporarily turned you into his 'inside man,' but now we've got an inside man of our own."

Devon squeezed her hand. "Rae, I love you, but hate it when you're being damn cryptic."

She looked Julian squarely in the eyes and smiled.

"How would you feel about going out on a little date with a pretty little girl in white; with wings, wears a halo?"

"There is no way in hell this is ever going to work." Julian was sitting on the bed back in his hotel room, the other four in a line before him, each giving their silent support.

"Of course it is!" Molly said quickly. "You just saw her last night! Why wouldn't you call to see her again? It's the perfect plan." Her brow furrowed. "By the way, why didn't you tell us that you saw her last night? And by us, I mean...*me*."

His eyes swept Molly caustically up and down. "Oh, I wonder."

"Jules," Rae said calmly, "it's going to work. Just tell her that you're going to be staying in town an extra day or two, and that you'd love to see her again before you head back to England."

"And be flexible," Devon handed him the phone. "Let her pick the time and place."

Julian rolled his eyes as he took it. "Asset acquisition 101; I know what I'm doing. I just," he trailed off nervously and glanced down at the phone, "I don't know if I can lie like that and be believable. This isn't just some mark."

Rae's face softened. "You don't want to hurt her."

"No," he said quickly, "I do, I mean, I want to *stop* her, it's just... She's going to hear it in my voice. I'm no good at this sort of thing."

"It's a relationship," Devon said simply. "She lied to you, you lie to her. It's as simple as that."

Rae cast him a disconcerted look. "Yeah, I'm filing that one away for later."

He rolled his eyes. "I meant it's a *work* relationship, the kind of tactics and espionage we've been trained for. She was playing you. Now you get to return the favor. Try not to think of her as your..." He stopped short at the look on Julian's face. "I just mean, try to think of her as an agent of Cromfield's. Nothing more."

Luke stepped forward. "If it helps, I could call and pretend to be you." He put on a ridiculous deep, brooding voice. "Meet me at the hotel...don't try to kill me... Pretty good, right?"

Even Julian had to smile at that one, and the mood was temporarily lightened. He dialed the first few numbers before turning, glancing up with one final concern. "She's good, guys. She's really good."

Molly rolled her eyes. "Honestly, Julian, enough. I like to be a busy body about your love life, but it's not like I want to know the details—"

"Her *ink*, Molls."

"Oh."

He spoke primarily to Rae, but addressed everyone. "If she gets her hands on you, even for a second, that's it! You're done. There's no fighting it."

Luke nudged Rae playfully. "Yeah, but we have Miss Super Hero over here. What's the worst that can happen?"

Rae beamed with pride, but Julian shook his head slowly. "Actually, I think our best bet is with Molly. Or with one of the abilities that Rae doesn't use very often."

Rae looked up curiously. "What do you mean? Which ones?"

Julian explained calmly, "Think of fighting her like fighting Kraigan. Except the second she touches you, she doesn't take just one of your abilities; she takes out all of them in one fell swoop."

For the first time all morning, nervous butterflies started battering against the walls of Rae's stomach. She remembered very well what it was like to fight Kraigan. He was a nightmare. And even though she'd managed to beat him last time in the parking lot, he'd still managed to get some of her powers along the way. From the sound of it, that wouldn't cut it with Angel.

"You can't hit her, you can't knock her down," Julian continued. "She might go flying, but she'll get back up and that'll be it for you. Devon, Luke, and I are basically out unless we try to take her down with something that won't bring us skin to skin. So that leaves you and Molly. Powers that can disarm without bringing you into direct contact. Electricity is great. You can also use wind, water...anything like that. Things that project."

"And all that's *if* she decides to go out on another date," Molly mumbled, looking a bit discouraged for the first time.

But the more he talked it out, the stronger Julian seemed to become. His eyes gleamed at the chance to right some of the wrongs that had been forced upon him, and he actually dialed the phone with a bit of a smile.

"You leave that part to me."

Chapter 12

It could not have been more awkward. Rae, Devon, Luke, and Molly stood in an uncomfortable circle while Julian sat on the edge of the bed, trying to ask his fake girlfriend to come over for sex.

Julian's fingers drummed nervously on the edge of the phone, and, when the line opened, Rae could have sworn he stopped breathing.

"Hello?"

The second he heard the seductive voice, his eyes snapped shut, but, when he spoke, he was collected and calm. "Hey, it's me."

"Julian? I thought you were heading back to England."

Rae gritted her teeth as she listened in with Devon's tatù. *The little liar probably gave that exact report to Cromfield when she crept out the window this morning.*

"Plans changed; I'm going to be here another day. Are you still in town? I'd love to see you again before the flight."

She giggled lightly. "I bet you'd love to see me again. I'd love to see you again, too. That was pretty intense last night. You've got a particular set of skills. Very impressive."

Julian bit his lip and glanced self-consciously at the ceiling, while the rest of them discreetly looked every other direction in an almost comical 'we're not here,' kind of way.

"Yeah," he kept his voice remarkably steady, "it was fun. So do you want to come back to the hotel? I could come to your place if you want. Meet in the middle? What sounds good to you?"

She paused, and, for a second, the entire room held their breath.

"Why don't you come to my place? I can open a bottle of wine. I'll change into the little pink thing you like. We can—"

"That's great," he said quickly, cutting her short. "Text me the address, and I'll head over."

There was another pause. "Are you...okay? You sound a little off."

Rae's heart caught in her chest.

But Julian spoke so smoothly, Rae almost believed him herself. "Sorry; it's just my friends." He lowered his voice, "They keep trying to get me to go out with them on a tour of the city. It's driving me friggin' crazy, and I can't stop thinking about you. And now that pink thing."

She laughed a clear pretty laugh that sounded nothing like the evil seductress Rae knew she was. It was a little creepy, being faced with the lie straight on. She could only imagine how Julian felt.

"Well, come to see me, baby, and I'll help you forget all about them."

His face tightened painfully and he looked down. "Okay; I'm on my way."

He went to hang up the phone, but she called out once more. "Jules...I love you."

He caught his breath, and Rae could have sworn a single tear fell down his face.

"I love you, too."

The address Angel texted Julian brought them to an apartment uptown. It was in a nicer neighborhood, mostly residential, while the opposite side of the building opened into a busy shopping center. Actually, the whole thing reminded Rae very much of the apartment waiting for her back in London, and she looked up at the skyscraper, jealously, from her place hidden in one of the stores.

The plan was simple.

All five friends would follow in behind Julian, invisible, and when they got close enough, both Molly and Rae would shock Angel at the same time. The only trick was that they all had to be touching to maintain invisibility, and that meant that Rae and Molly would have to detach at precisely the moment they fired off the lightning.

When phrased like that, it didn't seem so hard.

They'd been through worse. Hell, they'd been through much worse. And, Rae had to admit, it would be rather satisfying to get revenge on the girl who'd torn out her best friend's heart and stomped it all over the floor.

Except, the way Julian had warned them about Angel made her pause. She knew it wouldn't be that easy.

The second Julian opened the door, Rae sensed something was off.

All the curtains were closed in Angel's apartment, and, while that might be normal, considering the evening she had in mind, what wasn't normal was the way her eyes darted around the outside perimeter before coming to rest on Julian.

Rae had done that same visual sweep before. It wasn't cursory; it was tactical.

Then there was Angel herself.

Rae had to admit, as much as she hated the girl, Angel was *stunning*.

Long sheets of white-blond hair framed her creamy-skinned heart-shaped face; a face so pale in color it made her blue eyes jump out like little diamonds glittering in snow. Her lips were meticulously painted, and her body was slender, but fit. Knowing what she knew now, it wasn't hard for Rae to imagine this seemingly-delicate-looking girl springing suddenly into action or abruptly whipping out a gun.

"Hi," Julian said quietly, noting her minute hesitation just as Rae had. "Can I come in?" He smiled charmingly, and her face melted into an equally easy smile, dazzling them all with a row of perfect pearly teeth.

It's a shame she's such a psychopath, Rae thought to herself. *She and Julian would have made some beautiful children.*

"Of course," she purred, wrapping her arms around his neck and pulling him inside.

It was a gamble on both sides. He made sure to leave the door open so Rae and others could slip through unnoticed, but she kept her hands on him—meaning that Rae and Molly didn't dare shock her, for fear they'd get him as well.

"It's good to see you," he murmured with a believable smile. His eyes sparkled down as he took her arms and tried to gently remove them from around his neck.

She beamed back, but held fast, grinning as she stood up on her toes. "Likewise."

For a moment, neither one of them moved. The hands on the clock seemed to be stuck in place as Rae's eyes darted between them, wondering what to do.

Then, in a truly heartbreaking moment, Angel kissed Julian.

His head bent down to meet hers as her slender hands wove through his dark hair. Their eyes shut, and Rae realized, her own eyes prickling with tears, that the kiss was real.

Then Angel pulled away.

And Julian...didn't.

If only Rae had realized what was going on. If only she had understood a second sooner.

Julian wasn't lingering in the kiss.

He was frozen.

By the time she figured it out, so was she.

Angel had twirled in a wild spin, stretching her fingers into the air, when she'd caught the edge of Molly's arm. Unfortunately, with all four of them still connected, her deadly ink worked its magic on them all. Rae's group cloak of invisibility lifted immediately, and all four of them popped suddenly back into view, each with looks of identical shock. It was exactly like Julian had said.

It wasn't that Rae couldn't move—it was like she didn't remember how. She tried to focus very hard on her feet, willing them to somehow break free, but it was like trying to hold a fistful of water. The harder she tried, the more every ounce of control slipped right through her fingers.

"So," Angel stepped back with a little smirk, "this is the infamous gang. Let's see," she mocked as she stepped down the line, one by one. "You must be Molly. Little redhead, never stops talking, power to shock." She flicked the edge of one of Molly's fingers before she moved on. "Then we have dear old Devon, the best friend. Dean of Guilder's son. Golden boy of the Privy Council. Fennec fox tatù." She rolled up his sleeve and examined it curiously. "Cute."

Rae's blood boiled in her veins. This would be easy, huh? Five on one, huh? They'd been fools. There was a reason Cromfield had picked her. This girl was like walking Novocain.

"I think you must be Luke." Angel paused in front of him only briefly, just to check his arm before moving on. "No ink at all, so I'm not really sure what you're doing here." She stopped and glared at the last of the lineup. "And, of course, that brings us to the belle of the ball, Rae Kerrigan." She stared at Rae with a cocky grin. "Cromfield said to be careful of you. What a joke."

Rae wished she could grab the little tart and fling her across the room. Her stupid mouth wouldn't work either.

"So you're the one all the fuss is about..." Her eyes took on a hard glint as she reached out and flipped back one of Rae's curls. "I'm not going to lie, Kerrigan; it's kind of weird to finally be seeing you in person. I feel like you've been haunting me. You're all I hear about—day in, day out. You'd think you were a god or something. But, no, here you are, frozen just like the rest. Stupid little girl."

Rae glared at her. Stupid? Little girl? She had her mother's heart, but her father's temper. When this stupid freezing wore off, she was going to give this dark Angel a little taste of her own medicine.

Angel grinned again and took a step back to examine them as a group. "Julian's told me all about you guys, you see. Nothing sensitive, of course, nothing indiscreet. But you'd be surprised what a guy will say in the heat of the moment."

Rae felt as though she was going explode on the spot. Who the hell did this girl think she was?! First she uses Julian, and now here she was, rubbing it in his face?!

But a part of her didn't really believe that. The heart part. Rae had seen that kiss. It was real on both sides.

Angel had fallen for Julian just as honestly as he'd fallen for her.

"He really cares about each and every one of you," she said matter-of-factly. "Respects you." Her ice blue eyes flicked back to him with a hint of resentment. "He respects me, too, or at least I thought he did. So imagine my surprise when he brings all of you here to...what, honey?" She stroked the side of Julian's frozen face. "Take me down?"

Think, Rae, just think. There has to be a way out of this.

Like clockwork, she flipped through every tatù she had, one after another. Nothing worked. It was like her whole brain had been dipped in ice. It had simply stopped moving.

All at once, her heart skipped a beat.

Stopped moving? At a cellular level? Well, maybe there was a way to speed that back up.

Rather distracted by the sudden turn of events, Angel crossed the room to where her cell phone lay on the table. "Well, I'm not going to lie; I wasn't quite counting on this to happen. I know my boss obviously wants to meet you, but he wanted to get a few things ready first..."

As she paced back and forth, unsure what to do, Rae switched into the one and only tatù she had that was still working: Maria's telepathy. She sent out the message to everyone at once, ironically pleased that Luke, who had never had someone speak inside his head before, wasn't able to jump and give them all away.

Okay, guys, here's the plan. I'm not sure if this is actually going to work, and I can only use one tatù at a time. So here's what we're going to do. I'll count down from five. On the beat after, everyone hit the deck. Then, Molly, I want you to send out a shockwave like you've never done before, got it?

There was a pause.

Stay frozen if you got it.

Nothing like a little telepathic humor to lighten the mood.

In the background, Angel finally began dialing her phone to call Cromfield. It was now or never.

Okay, on five...four...three...two...one...NOW!

In a flash, Rae switched from Maria's tatù to Camille's—sending out a blast of super-speed vibrations throughout the air.

It worked!

It freakin' worked!

Angel's ink obviously took effect on a molecular level, slowing things down. When applied correctly, Camille's could literally shake it loose. Just as Rae sent out the blast, she hit the deck, covering her head in the same instant.

Except...nothing happened.

Molly—now!

Nothing.

There was a gasp of shock, and Rae slowly opened one eye then the other. She cautiously lifted her head half an inch to see Angel's boots standing in front of her.

Before she could raise her head the rest of the way, a vicious kick in the ribs made her double over in pain. She flew back with a piercing cry until she hit something hard and came to an abrupt stop.

It was Devon, she realized with a start. Still frozen. They were all still frozen, standing in a line behind her. Her brilliant freakin' plan had apparently only worked on her.

She reached up and grabbed handfuls of his jacket, half-apologizing to him as she pulled herself to her feet. With a frustrated sigh, Angel came at her again.

"How the hell are you still moving?" she demanded furiously, tossing back her white-blond hair and storming across the room.

Rae's eyes glittered as she relished what was sure to come. "Guess this little girl's not as stupid as all the rest of them." Acting instinctively, her body switched into Jennifer's tatù. She angled herself half behind Devon, and brought her lips down to his ear as she whispered, "I'm sorry about this, too, babe."

A disgusted expression floated across Angel's face. "Hiding behind the boyfriend? Really? Even I wouldn't do that."

Rae cocked her head and glared. "Well, you wouldn't really have the option, would you? Seeing as Julian was never really your boyfriend." She was taunting Angel, trying to get her to come just close enough, but she meant the words with all her heart. This girl was going to pay for what she'd done to Julian. She was going to pay for it right now.

The second Angel stepped within range, Rae leapt into the air, spinning around using Devon's neck—sending her body rocketing forward. She kicked Angel squarely in the chest, feeling the impotent hum as Angel tried to freeze her again before smashing into the sofa across the room.

Damn cushions, Rae thought as Angel pulled herself up and sprinted back across the room.

But, this time, the tables had turned. Angel might be able to freeze, but Rae could shake it.

Furthermore, Rae was suddenly able to freeze people...

"What are you—" Angel's voice cut off in surprise as she suddenly stopped in place, a curling fist still wound up behind her head. For a moment, her eyes dilated in fear, but then she focused herself and broke free—using her childhood mastery of the ability to shake it off. "You *stole* my ink!"

Rae smirked, walking slowly towards her. "Well, usually I ask permission first, but seeing what a raging bitch you were to my friend...I decided just to go for it." She held up her hands thoughtfully as the new tatù hummed through her skin. "But, thanks, Angel. It's not one of my best, but I'm sure it's bound to come in handy."

Angel's eyes flashed ice blue. "No ink, then. Just you and me."

"I can't think of anything better."

With a muted crash, they came together. Fists flying. Legs kicking. Eyes flashing as they fell in a tangled heap on the floor. Angel was not nearly as delicate as she looked. The second they landed on the carpet, she knocked Rae's jaw back with enough force that a pool of blood flooded her mouth. Rae spat it out and countered with a punch of her own, catching Angel right below the eye.

"Just...stay...down!" Angel cried, tugging on Rae's hair and kneeing her in the face.

Rae collapsed to the floor but spun around in a wide kick, taking Angel down with her. "You know," she panted, elbowing Angel in the eye, "we should have known it was you." She struggled to break free of a chokehold. "You are so...not...Julian's...type!"

They broke apart with a scream and came back together again.

This time, the fighting got dirtier, the tatù rule instantly forgotten when Angel temporarily froze Rae as she scrambled backwards. But she had barely gotten to her feet before Rae shook it off and launched herself forward in a gust of wind, sending them both crashing through a nearby coffee table.

Both girls cried out as they landed in the pile of broken glass, and, for a moment, there was a brief truce. Rae bit her lip to stop from crying as she pulled a huge shard out of her hand. On the other side of the room, Angel was doing the same thing, extracting the razor-sharp shrapnel from her leg. Molly, Devon, Julian, and Luke were still standing in a frozen line, watching the battle unfold.

For the briefest of moments, Rae looked up and met Devon's lovely eyes. They might have been frozen in place, but it was easy to see the pain there, the overwhelming helpless fury of watching from the sidelines, unable to help.

I'm fine, Dev, she said telepathically. *I'm fine.*

But even as she thought the words, they suddenly couldn't be less true.

There was a soft *click*. Soft but unmistakable.

One little sound, but it changed everything.

Rae's heart stopped in her chest as she rotated slowly d.

It was a gun, alright. But Angel wasn't pointing it at her—she was pointing it straight at Devon's chest.

"Angel, wait—"

"Not a word, Kerrigan," Angel interrupted, steadying her hand. "And I know all about your little powers. Try anything, he's dead. Disappear, he's dead. You might be fast, Rae, but you're not faster than a bullet."

Rae's face paled as she wondered whether that was strictly true. Either way, it wasn't like she could take the chance. And, from where she stood, she couldn't reach Devon. She could only reach Julian.

Wait...*Julian.*

Her heart started tentatively beating as she slowly reached out her hand. That might just be enough.

"I said don't—"

But Rae had already unfrozen him, using Camille's ability to shake the freeze loose.

His head came back up slowly, finally released from his unending kiss, and his dark eyes locked on Angel. It was impossible to say who looked more devastated, who looked more betrayed. But from the moment he was free, there was something else there as well. Cold, hard determination.

"Angel," he said softy.

Her hand trembled on the gun.

"You're not going to shoot my best friend."

Her eyes flickered to him for the briefest of moments before returning to Rae, carefully monitoring her behavior.

"I can't just let you go, Jules. You don't understand. Cromfield will—" Her voice choked off in sudden fear before dropping to a low murmur. "I can't just let you go."

Julian calmly ignored this, taking a step between Devon and the gun.

"Jules. Stay back," she warned.

Another step.

"I'm warning you—I'll shoot!" her voice shook, slightly, but she stood her ground. "Don't make me shoot!"

But Julian positioned his body between them, staring down the barrel of the gun with the same steady determination that he did everything else in his life.

"If you want to shoot him, you'll have to shoot through me," he answered calmly. Whether or not he thought she might actually do that, it was impossible to tell. But, by now, the gun was full-on shaking; a shaking that only got worse as Julian started walking towards her.

"Julian...please," she whispered.

The gun was almost touching his chest now, but he didn't give it a second glance. His eyes were only on Angel. "Put it down," he said softly, his voice as low as hers. "Angel...just let it go. It's over."

There was a wretched cry, and the gun suddenly fell to the floor. It hit the carpet with a dull thud as Angel's eyes welled over with tears. She didn't look at anyone. It was like she didn't dare. But Rae still kept a close eye on her as she walked over and quickly unfroze the rest of her friends.

There was a sudden flash of electric blue, followed by a piercing scream.

"Molly!" Rae cried, whipping her head around.

At the same time, Julian shouted, "Angel!"

By the time Rae looked up, Julian was on his feet and tearing towards his lying girlfriend. She had been thrown up against the wall, breaking the plaster, and her clothes were still smoking as a little trickle of blood slipped down from her hair.

"Jules, don't touch her!" Devon commanded, stumbling a little as the inescapable freeze cleared from his system.

Julian paused half an inch away, but gathered her up in his arms anyway, staring down at her unconscious body with a mixture of utter devastation and remorse. With trembling hands, he wiped away the smear of blood, lowering his lips to her ear and whispering, "I'm sorry." The others gave him a minute, looking away until he finally let her go and got to his feet.

Once he was clear, Devon walked forward cautiously. He clapped Julian quickly on the shoulder, casually turning him the other way in the process, as he picked up Angel himself and carried her to a nearby chair. His eyes flicked up to Rae in a silent request, and she walked forward, conjuring a thick rope as she did. Devon looped it expertly around the sleeping girl, careful not to touch her in the process. Once he was sure it was secure, he turned back to Julian, a little uncomfortable as to how to proceed.

"Jules," he murmured, "maybe you want to step outside for this."

Julian's eyes flashed to Devon's before coming to rest on Angel. It was impossible to say what he was thinking. Even his closest friends, who had known him for so many years, were at a complete loss.

"No," he said quietly, "I'm going to stay." Then a little louder, "Devon, get whatever information we need, but..."

Devon nodded solemnly. "I won't."

There was a sudden vibration behind them, and the five of them turned as one to see a cell phone buzzing on the coffee table. Luke, the closest one, picked it up. A very strange expression flitted across his face as he held it out to Rae.

"It's...it's him."

Rae and Devon shared a quick look.

"Rae, don't take—"

But she'd already picked it up.

"Angel," a deep voice spoke sharply from the other end, "I don't know why you wanted to linger in San Francisco, but I'm still waiting for—"

"Angel's dead."

The words were out of Rae's mouth before she'd even considered speaking them. Her friends were staring at her in horrified amazement, but it was as if she suddenly knew exactly what to say.

"But don't worry—I'm sure you'll be seeing her soon."

There was a chilling pause on the other end, and then a deep chuckling.

"Well played, my dear, well played. I'm not going to pretend I'm pleased about Angel...she was an invaluable help to me with your friend. I have to say, I didn't know you had it in you."

Rae's voice was pure ice. "I'm sure it won't be the first time you underestimate me."

Cromfield cleared his throat, and Rae got the feeling he was angrier than he was letting on.

"Listen, Rae, I'm sure in time you're going to—"

"No, you listen." She gripped the phone so hard against her head, she worried it might break. "This is what happens. You send people after me, they die. You come after me or my friends, or any other hybrids for that matter—and you're next. You wanted to play? Then we're going to play. Do you hear me, you sick son of a—"

The phone was ripped from her hand and smashed against the floor.

She looked up in shock, to see Devon staring at her with a truly unreadable look on his face.

A feeling of recklessness akin to guilt welled up in her chest, but, before she could say anything, there was a faint stirring on the chair, and all five of them watched on pins and needles as Angel slowly came to. At first, she looked merely confused as to why she was sitting down, then her eyes travelled up to see all of them glaring back at her.

Her gaze came to rest on Julian. "So..." the side of her lips came up in a sad smile, "you know."

He said nothing, his arms folded tightly across his chest.

"Since when did you know?" she continued. "Before the other night?"

"No," he snapped at her suddenly. "I wouldn't have done that if I'd known."

A look of deep hurt flashed momentarily in her eyes before she cleared her expression and nodded practically. "Yeah, if I was in your shoes, I guess I wouldn't have either."

"Why did Cromfield leave Benjamin Mills alive?" Devon was all business; no time for emotional confessions or deep catharsis here.

Her eyes flashed to him with a hint of frustration before returning to Julian. It was to him that she answered, even though he hadn't asked the question. "He doesn't need to kill hybrids anymore."

Devon scoffed. "Really?"

Angel kept her eyes still on Julian. "He doesn't need to kill them to get what he needs. In fact, he hasn't in a long time. Not since scientists discovered the concept of DNA in the 1950s. Now he only needs a sample."

Rae stepped forward. "A sample? Why?" Cromfield wanted hybrids dead. Taking samples of them made absolutely no sense. She glared at Angel. "I said, why?" Rae didn't care what sort of inner heartbreak this girl may be trying to hide. It was Julian's heartbreak she cared about. And the dozens of hybrid lives that this sick experiment of Cromfield's had claimed.

Angel shrugged. "Beats me."

Devon nodded calmly, but he was staring at Angel with pure hate. "Julian told you everything about me, right? Told you that I've risked my life for him? That I think of him as my brother?"

She stared at him uncertainly, not sure where this was going.

When she didn't say anything, Devon stepped forward with the most chilling expression Rae had ever seen on his face. "Knowing that, do you think there is realistically anything I won't do to the girl who broke his heart? Do you think there's any line I won't cross?" His voice dropped to a lethal whisper as he leaned down to her ear. "I don't have to touch you for you to feel it."

Julian's face tightened and he looked away.

If it was possible, Angel grew even paler than before. And when Julian refused to meet her eyes, she looked up at Devon with a sigh. "He has a list of ingredients he's combining with hybrid DNA. Ethanol, midazolam, and sodium pentothal. He's mixing it together to make some kind of serum. I don't know what it does."

"Wait." Molly frowned. "He's using the hybrids to make the serum? He's not giving it to them?"

Angel tossed her blood-matted hair out of her face. "Well, he mixed my blood in with a tranquilizer to subdue some of the feistier ones, but, no; they're not the intended recipients."

"Then who is?" Devon asked sharply.

Her eyes flicked up with a trace of fear before she said, "I don't know. All I know is that he's collecting different samples and mixing them together. And that he's crazy obsessed with your girlfriend." She stifled a shudder and murmured, "And that he's going to kill me for telling you this."

There was a sudden movement on the other side of the room as Julian slid down into a chair, unable to watch any longer. Her eyes went to him and she tried to get up before remembering the ropes.

"Jules," she called softly.

"Don't you dare," Molly snapped. "Don't you dare talk to him."

Angel stared past her to Julian. "Jules, I'm sorry. When I met you in Florence, I... This is what my family has always done, Julian. For over five hundred years. I didn't want it to involve you. I'm sorry it did." She bowed her head. "I'm sorry for everything. I never wanted to hurt you."

He met her eyes for only the briefest of moments before fixing his stare on the wall. "What a beautiful speech..."

All at once, as strange as it might be, Rae knew what she had to do. Her friend was not going to recover from this. Was not going to get over the fact that the only girl he'd ever fallen in love with was only pretending to love him back. It would completely destroy him.

And it wasn't even true...

Squaring her shoulders, she walked quickly across the room, kneeling down in front of Angel's chair with a look of pure determination.

"Rae, what're you doing?" Devon asked nervously. "Get back."

Keeping Angel fixed in her gaze the whole time, she slowly reached out her hand.

"Rae! Get back! Don't let her touch you!"

But Rae was calm, leaning forward so only Angel could hear. "I'm going to give you one chance to leave him less broken than how you made him. When I touch your skin, I'll know the truth. He's seen me do it before, and he'll believe what I say." She swallowed and stared hard at Angel. "I also know how to break your freezing ability, so it's useless to try it on me."

Angel's eyes grew wide as they fixed on Rae's hand. She didn't say anything, but Rae got the feeling that she'd just thrown out a life preserver and Angel was ready to grab on.

They were almost touching, when Rae suddenly paused. "If you try to freeze me, I'm going to let my three friends cheerfully beat you to death. And Julian will never know the truth."

Angel nodded, serious as could be. "I won't freeze you."

Still aware of the fact that she might be making a huge mistake, Rae grabbed Angel's cold hand in her own. She almost gasped aloud at the rush of feelings that was waiting for her. Fear, bewilderment, betrayal. A young girl apprenticed to a never-aging man, forced to watch and do terrible things.

Instead of using Ellie's power like she'd planned, her body slipped into Carter's power, seeing down into the very depths of Angel's soul. There was tragedy there, more than there was light. But none of it seemed to be her fault.

Rae saw a young white-haired girl taken out of her mother's arms. She saw flashes of that same girl growing up, living mostly on the move or in St. Stephen's cemetery underground. Saw glimpses of her crying as she tried to fall asleep, covering her ears to the echoing screams of different hybrids in the next room.

And then, as dark as everything was before, it suddenly changed.

For the first time, Rae saw Julian standing on a bridge in Florence, staring confusedly at a map. Rae's heart, as Angel's, soared as she went over to make her introduction. She felt the faint stirrings of real happiness for the first time as Julian looked at her and smiled. Felt the way her heart melted every time they kissed, and shattered into a million pieces every time she went back to report to Cromfield.

She was in love. From the bottom of her broken heart. There was no denying it.

When Rae finally ripped her hand away with a gasp, there were tears in her eyes; the same tears she saw running down Angel's face.

"Please," Angel whispered, "take care of him for me. Keep him safe."

Still trembling, Rae got to her feet. Devon was there in an instant to see if she was okay, but she turned instead to Julian, who was watching her with wide, apprehensive eyes. Without saying a word, she walked slowly towards him and pulled him to his feet.

Then she held out her hand, and conjured a knife.

His eyes flashed up to hers in horror. "Rae, you can't—"

She shook her head at his misconception and handed the knife to him. "Untie her."

"WHAT?!"

The word echoed at the same time from Molly, Luke, and Devon, who were all staring at Rae as if she'd lost her mind. Julian, however, was looking at her with the faintest bit of hope.

"She loves you, Jules," Rae smiled faintly. "She always has. I think she probably always will."

A small light shone deep in his eyes as he strode across the room, and, with one skilled slice, cut her ropes from her. She got to her feet in a daze, staring up at him with tears in her eyes.

"Jules, I—"

He silenced her with a kiss. This one was very different from the first.

It wasn't an ending.

It wasn't a last goodbye.

It was only the beginning.

He pulled back, barely breathing, touching his forehead lightly against hers. "You need to run now. You can't go back to Cromfield, and the PC won't take you in, not after what you've done."

She nodded quickly, still smiling, unwilling to take her gaze from his face. "But you? You would be willing to—"

He kissed her again before picking up her coat and putting it on her shoulders. "Go," he said softly. "Keep yourself safe. Do that for me. One day I'll find you. Heaven help me, but I'll find you."

She stared at him for one final second before nodding and gathering up her things. She cast the others a look of farewell and squeezed Rae's hand in a silent thank-you as she headed for the door. Taking a deep breath, she pulled it open and was about to leave, when Julian suddenly said,

"Angel..."

She turned around and their eyes met.

He watched her for a second before his lips turned up in a sparkling smile. "I'll know where to find you."

Her face broke out into a smile of its own before she nodded again and vanished through the open door.

"Yes, but how did you *know* she wouldn't freeze you?" Luke slurred, peering through the glass of the empty bottle. "What if you had gotten stuck like that forever?"

The five of them were sitting in the hotel lounge, recovering from the emotional roller coaster of the day. They'd tried using Angel's phone to find Cromfield, but it had a protective thumb print which they obviously didn't have, and then Molly had zapped it by mistake in frustration. There was no other way to find him, nor did they actually want to. So they headed back to the hotel.

Luke and Molly were comfortably intertwined, Julian was practically glowing from happiness, and Rae had recently discovered the wonders of 'hard root beer' and was happily guzzling it by the pint.

"I just did," she hiccupped, and shrugged. "You can't fake a kiss like that."

"It was a huge risk," Devon said quietly. He alone was not partaking in their fun, choosing instead to watch it from afar, his chair tilted slightly away.

Rae hiccupped again. "No different than the risks we usually take."

His eyes met hers, and she got the feeling that maybe that was the point. But before he could answer, Molly stuck her glass under Rae's open hand. "Beer me."

Luke raised his eyebrows and chuckled. "*Beer* you?"

"What?" She shrugged. "I heard it on TV once; I'm ninety-nine percent sure it's a thing that people say."

Julian laughed, sipping down his whiskey. "Frat boys and douche bags say 'beer me,' Molls."

"Oh, yeah?" Rae raised her eyebrows. "Well, then, how *you* would know?"

"I must have seen it on the same show," he teased.

In rather drunken concentration, Rae covered the top of Molly's glass with her hand, and it filled with a frothy amber liquid. "Tell me how you like that one," she said seriously. "I tried to make it sweeter than the rest."

Molly took a huge gulp and grinned. "Much better. I'm not going to lie, Rae, you totally suck at food. But beer and coffee? You're the best."

Luke laughed aloud and gathered her up in his arms. "Imagine the trouble the two of you could get into if you weren't out saving the world every night."

Devon sighed softly, but Luke didn't hear him. "Maybe it's a good thing that you're so consistently distracted."

"Well," Molly grinned, "we're not going to be saving the world for long!"

Rae leaned forward excitedly. "Are you thinking what I'm thinking?"

"Um—how Angel's apartment looked almost exactly like ours, and how I'm so excited to finally get to live in it, and how we're going to see it by the end of tomorrow, and how I totally forgot but totally just remembered that it's also right by that sushi place we love so much?"

Rae's jaw dropped open in amazement. "Yes! I was thinking all of those things!"

Molly leaned back with a superior shrug. "It's because we're best friends. We don't even need Maria's telepathy. We just have it."

"Oh, yeah! That was another thing!" Luke exclaimed, just remembering. "You freakin' *spoke in my head*, Rae. How crazy was that?!"

Molly patted him indulgently on the knee as Rae grinned. "He's so new to all of this. He's like a little baby!"

Rae cracked up, turning to Devon. "Do you remember when I was like that, babe? So innocent and naïve. And *charming*! Can we talk about how *charming* I was?"

Devon pushed suddenly to his feet. "I'm going to bed. See you guys tomorrow." He left before they could say anything, and Rae and the rest of them stared at his retreating back in shock.

A heavy sinking feeling stirred in the pit of Rae's stomach, and she rubbed her eyes, already dreading the conversation she knew was sure to come.

Molly turned to her with concern. "Was it something I said?"

"No," Rae assured her quickly, pushing to her feet as well. "No, this was all me."

Chapter 13

"You're angry with me," Rae said the words the second she opened the door, leaning back against it as the hard root beer slowly cleared from her system. She used Charles' tatù to sober up the rest of the way, making a mental note to remember to use that in the future.

Devon sat fully dressed in the center of the bed. He'd been staring at the ceiling when she came in, but looked up the second he heard her voice. "I'm angry with you," he repeated her words exactly, keeping his voice an even tone.

Rae sighed and pushed her hair out of her face before joining him on the mattress. "Can I ask why? Or do you just want to stew in it for a while?"

He sat quietly for a moment before casting her a sideways glance. "You know, I've only been frozen a couple times before today."

She frowned, thrown off balance. "What?"

"When I first joined up with the PC and was in training, they made me train with a new recruit. She got me." He shuddered as he remembered. "I could handle it better then because I knew counting down the freeze time would set me free. The new recruit was cute; that helped as well." He smiled briefly at their shared memory in the Oratory and then frowned. "But I hated it. I don't know if it hit me so hard because I have a tatù based on movement, or what, but today I felt like the longer I stayed trapped there, the more a part of me just died." He bowed his head.

Although Rae was pretty damn sure that the two of them were in a fight, she reached over and rubbed his back, comfortingly. "I'm sorry," she said softly. "I felt like that, too. Angel's ink is—"

"It had nothing to do with Angel's ink," he interrupted, turning to look at her full on. "It had everything do to with you."

She shook her head blankly, mentally forbidding herself to use Carter's power to find out what the hell was going on inside his head. "Devon, I don't understand what you—"

"Why did you touch her?" he suddenly exclaimed. "A girl who just seconds before was dialing the man who wants to take you away from me! Why did you let Julian cut her loose when you couldn't be one hundred percent sure she wouldn't change her mind? Why is it that whenever someone dangerous comes after you, you head straight for them? *Why do you always have to run into every dangerous room first?*"

"I'm just protecting you."

"I don't need you to protect me! That's my job!" His head dropped down into his hands as his shoulders fell with a tired sigh. "I'm doing everything I can to keep you, Rae. Fighting on all fronts. But you just go tearing right into it. It's like you don't care if we have a future—"

"Devon... I have nothing *but* future." She didn't want to have this talk. Not now and now ever. Certainly not yet. But it seemed the moment was upon them. There was no holding it back any longer. "What exactly are you fighting for?" she asked harshly, her words hissing in the air between them. "Do you realize that we'll never grow old together? Never grow up? If we ever had a kid—its name would go onto a list like the one we've been chasing. Hell, I probably can't have kids, that's how messed up my life is!" She shook her head, her hair swinging. "My life? It will be anything but sweet. We'll spend the next seventy years together as you get to experience life and I just bide the time. You'll count the seconds we have together, and I'll be counting the seconds until we're apart and I'm alone."

He opened his mouth, but she wouldn't let him talk.

"How's it going to be? In forty years, you'll be all grey, married to a teenager—hiding out in Texas. You'd have to start telling people you were my father! Then my grandfather!" Her voice sped up the longer she talked, winding her up into a panic. "Do you get all that? Do you get that we can't have a future together when only one of us *has* a future?"

He let her speak, let her give her little speech, but it didn't seem to matter to him in the slightest. When she was finished, he simply took her hand and held it tightly in his own. "We're going to figure it out."

She shot him an exasperated sigh. "Devon, how can you be so—?"

"What, Rae? So stupid? So optimistic? So incredibly naïve?" He knelt on the floor in front of the bed, leaning his arms on top of her legs. "Rae, you are the most powerful person I've ever met in my life. Maybe even the most powerful person who's ever walked the planet. Do you really think there's a problem out there that you and I can't fix?"

"Not when that problem is the fact that I won't die!"

In a rage that bordered on hysteria, she strode over to the desk and reached inside until she found a letter opener. Ignoring the look on Devon's face, she slashed it across her skin in a wide gash. For a second, it bled. For just a second, she was a just like everyone else. Then, with an efficiency that was almost disturbing, it started to close shut. Charles' tatù. Except she knew, even if she didn't have that ink, she would still heal.

The next second, she let herself fall on the floor, weeping.

Devon gathered her up in his arms and carried her to the bed, keeping a steady pressure on her arm even though it had already healed. He rocked her gently back and forth as she wept against his chest, staining his shirt with her tears.

"I just found you," she gasped, closing her eyes and holding him tighter. "I just found you and now you're getting taken away. And there's nothing either one of us can do about it."

"Just calm down, Rae; I'm not going anywhere," he whispered into her hair. "Just calm down and breathe."

But she couldn't stop. All the dark thoughts this month-long road-trip had kept at bay came tumbling out, snowballing into something big enough that she was crushed beneath it.

"Lanford, Kraigan, Jennifer, your father, my uncle, the Privy Council itself; everyone has always been against us, Devon, and it hasn't mattered. But *this*? What can we do about this?"

"I don't know," he said softly.

She pulled away and stared at him. Despite the uncertainty of the words, he didn't seem completely devastated like she was. He wasn't falling apart at the seams. Instead, he was still staring at her with that calm, open smile. Holding her hand like it was the simplest thing in the world.

"I don't know what's going to happen," he said steadily. "I can't know the future. I can only know where we've been. Rae, you've said it yourself: Two people have never accomplished so much, never jumped through as many hurdles as we have just to stay together. Our love has survived in the face of unspeakable odds. Held up against attacks from all sides—good and evil."

With a calm assuredness that threatened to break through her panic, he leaned in and kissed her softly on the lips.

"When I say 'we're going to get through this,' I'm not putting you off. I mean it with all my heart. We're going to figure this out, Rae. If anyone in the world can do it, it's us. You just have to trust in that." He kissed the tip of her nose with a playful smile. "Can you do that for me?"

She pulled in a shaky breath and nodded, curling up into him. "I can do that. I want to do that."

"Rae..." he murmured, lifting her up and sliding them both into bed.

"Yeah?"

"Can you also take it easy with the letter opener?"

When Rae woke up the next day, feeling slightly groggy but immensely relieved to have gotten the whole 'immortality' thing out with Devon, she woke up alone. She felt along the indented sheets, only to have her fingers stumble upon a wrinkled note.

Up early working at the library
Come and get me before the flight
Love you...

"What?" she mumbled. Today was the day they were supposed to head back to England in chains. What the hell was Devon doing at the public library?

Shrugging it off as one of the mysteries of her already-mysterious boyfriend, Rae conjured a toothbrush and a straightening iron, and headed to the bathroom. Fifteen minutes later, she emerged. Her dark hair, already long while curled, hung down to her waist—swinging back and forth in a shiny wave as she walked. She hardly ever wore it this way, but today was a special occasion.

Today was the day she was going to have to convince her mother, Carter, Devon's father, and whatever other angry adults were waiting for them back in England that she and her friends were more helpful alive and fighting than just following orders all the time. They were grown-ups now, for bloody sake.

To do this, she was going to have to look the part.

A frantic knock at her door made her think that maybe Molly was thinking the same thing.

"Molls? That you?"

"Clothing emergency!"

"Yeah, I hear you."

She opened the door and let her panicked friend inside. Molly had already gotten through a full-length rant on the merits of Prada versus Gucci before she stopped and noticed Rae's hair.

"Ooh, this is cute! What made you straighten it?"

"We need to look responsible," Rae answered, leading to stand in front of the bed. "We need to make it look like we didn't just take off on a whim, but that we were doing the right thing. That we can be trusted. Remind them how that trust was earned."

Molly nodded, biting her lip. "And really hope that they don't put us back on probation."

"Yes," Rae agreed hastily. "That, too. So, what do you think?"

Focusing all her concentration on a single design, she waved her hand rhythmically over the bed, and a simple lavender dress appeared. It was modest, falling to just below the knees with a high neckline, but stylish, too. The sleeves were cut in the Grecian style, and there was a little dip in the front that tied up with soft ribbons. Rae was pretty sure she'd seen something like it in one of Molly's magazines, but she was perfectly willing to take credit for it herself.

"Oh, Rae, that's perfect!" Molly held it up against her best friend and leaned back appraisingly. "Yeah, it's going to look even better with your hair like this." She jumped up and down in sudden glee. "Do you know that this means? Do you realize that, with this new tatù, we can literally do this every day back in England? It's like playing dress-up the way I always wanted to as a child!"

"With super-powers?" Rae asked doubtfully.

"Actually, yes."

Rae grinned. "So what about you?"

Molly was suddenly all business. "Okay, I'm glad you asked. I actually have something very specific in mind..."

Twenty minutes later, both girls headed down the stairs to meet up with the others in the lobby. Molly had opted for the preppy look, going with a black pleated skirt, black stockings, a white silk blouse, and a stylish women's tie. For a while, she had toyed around with the idea of a beret, but Rae had fortunately talked her out of it.

Julian waved hello when they got down to the lobby, looking rather dapper himself in newly- pressed clothes, and Luke jumped to his feet to pull out their chairs.

"Well, look at you ladies. All dressed up."

He kissed Molly swiftly on the cheek before handing both girls a coffee.

"What's this?" Molly asked in surprise.

He shrugged. "We didn't want Rae to think we were taking advantage of her new conjuring power, so we decided to buy it ourselves. You know, not take it for granted and stuff."

Molly and Rae exchanged a quick guilty look before turning away with identical grins.

"Yeah, we wouldn't want to take advantage..." Molly murmured into her cup.

"Where's Devon?" Julian asked, setting down the paper and coming over to join them.

Rae shook her head. "I was actually hoping he'd already be down here with you. I got a note from him this morning saying he was working at the library. No idea what that means..."

Julian rolled his eyes and slipped on his coat. "Devon's a freak. He gets an idea into his head and it has to be done *right* then. Doesn't matter if it's four in the morning."

Rae grinned and jumped up to ruffle his hair. "You speaking from experience?"

He chuckled and shook his head. "Yeah, it's made being partnered with him a real blast, let me tell you." He tried to ruffle her hair back, but Molly's hand shot out of nowhere and shocked him away.

"We *don't* touch the hair," she thundered, blowing the smoke off her fingers. "It's a rule."

Julian grimaced, flexing his fingers to regain feeling. "But she just—"

"Doesn't matter," Molly said solemnly. "Not ever."

He and Rae shared a muted grin before laughing out loud as they headed outside and down the street towards the library. "You're lucky your boyfriend is here, Molls," Julian said with a smile.

She jutted up her chin. "Oh yeah, and why's that?"

"Because if he weren't, I would pick you up and dump you right into that fountain."

Molly walked on the other side of Luke from then on.

When Devon had said he was at the library, Rae had pictured some small, childhood approximation. Either that, or the library at Guilder—a long, rectangular building full of endless cherry-wood tables and rows after rows of shelves. She had never once imagined something like the San Francisco Public Library.

Her eyes widened in awe as they stepped under the high, domed ceilings. Walls of sparkling white circled around and around, stacked what looked to be fifty feet high with books. Small groups of hushed people scurried past, each one darting to and fro as if their lives depended on it, and in the center of it all, a woman who looked strongly reminiscent of Madame Elpis hissed for quiet.

Strangely enough, it reminded her a bit of the Oratory back at Guilder. She absentmindedly wondered what it would be like to dangle from those rafters.

Using Elpis' own tatù, she spotted Devon on the fourth floor, and led her friends quickly up the stairs to meet him.

"Great time for you to decide you want a library card," she teased gently as they made their way around the curb. "Seriously, Dev, our flight's in like—"

She cut off quickly when she saw that he was actually in deep discussion with a white-haired, spindly-looking man with thick, horn-rimmed glasses. The man was pointing down to one of the many books Devon had scattered on the table around him, and Devon was hanging on every word with a thoughtful frown.

When he spotted his friends standing a short way behind, he clapped the old man on the shoulder and thanked him gratefully for his time. The man smiled, seemingly delighted to have had such an in-depth discussion. He waved farewell and headed off down the hall as Rae and her friends approached the table with care.

"You've certainly been," she let one of the weighty books drop with a thud, "busy."

They were stacked eight- or nine-high, threatening the very stability of the table. Julian picked one of them up with a frown. "Advanced redox reactions?" He dropped it as well. "You're studying chemistry?"

Devon sat down in the center, completely undaunted by their skepticism. "That man who just left? He's a world-renowned chemist from Oxford. I saw a poster taped up next to the hotel, that he'd be giving a lecture here last this morning, so I got up early to see it. Then, I started doing a little reading..."

Molly pursed her lips and perched upon the mountain of books. "A little. Sure."

Devon's eyes were wide and dilated, running fast on fumes as he continued. "You remember what Angel told us? That Cromfield was mixing bits of hybrid DNA with a combination of ethanol, midazolam, and sodium pentothal? Well, I was talking to the professor about it—leaving out the whole hybrid bit, of course—and he showed me a couple possible combinations of reactions."

Almost clumsy in his rush, he pulled out several hand-drawn formulas from a piece of paper half buried beneath a book about equilibria.

"Here! Look at this."

He thrust the paper in front of them, and their eyes glazed over as they scanned down the page. It was a bunch of gibberish, nothing more. With Devon's eager face waiting in front of them, Molly elbowed Rae automatically in the ribs.

"This better be good, Devon," she said, switching into Ellie's tatù. "Our flight leaves in three hours..."

But as her skin adjusted to the new ability with a warm buzz, her mouth fell open in shock as she looked again at the page. It wasn't just gibberish to her now, a random assortment of numbers and letters; it was a beautifully balanced equation. A formula of some sort, and by the way it was delicately arranged, she could tell it must have taken countless tries to get right.

"He's not making the serum to give to anyone other than himself," she breathed, studying the list of chemicals as she scanned down the page.

Devon shook his head firmly. "It's a mimic. A massive DNA absorption and balancing act, mixed in with a good number of neural inhibitors to fade after the initial transition."

"A mimic?" Molly asked in surprise. "What do you mean the serum's a mimic? Like Rae?"

Rae leaned back on her heels. "He's mimicking my copy-cat ability. Trying to recreate it by adding little bits of everyone he's come across. He can't absorb people's tatùs just by touch like I can, but, if he gets this right—and it looks like maybe he already has—he'll be able to permanently absorb their powers by getting a simple DNA sample."

Julian's face paled as he considered the possibilities. "So we're not just talking about another psychic with some outstanding longevity here..."

"...we're talking about another me."

Not another Kieran, or her father, but another full-fledged, full-tatù-abilitied copycat.

The group fell silent as the enormity of this discovery slowly took hold. On the one hand, it was almost a relief. No longer did they have to worry about the lives of the hybrids on the list. From this century on, there would be no more barbaric experiments, no more grisly deaths in rooms buried far beneath the earth. Aside from losing a piece of hair, people could go on living just as they had before, with their abilities safely intact.

On the other hand, Cromfield would have them as well. Who knew how many he'd already acquired, Rae thought with a fright. He'd been collecting bits and pieces of people since the time of Henry VIII. By now, he could be virtually unstoppable—as if his immortality hadn't already rendered that a moot point.

"So, then, why the breeding?" Luke asked quietly. The others turned to him in confusion, and he elaborated. "The pictures we saw in the catacombs. All those mothers, people forced to have children against their will, the mixing of tatùs. What was the point?"

Rae smiled wryly. "The point is that single tatùs tend to repeat over the generations. Molly has her dad's, Devon has his dad's, and his grandma's before that. There's a limited variety of 'standard' ink. By forcing people to breed hybrids, especially people with especially volatile tatùs, he was increasing his list to choose from. Making himself the ultimate power."

"We need to get this back to Carter," Devon said quietly. His voice had taken on a tone of soft panic. "We need to get the entire Privy Council in on this right away."

"Well," Molly said, "our flight leaves in three hours. Next stop, London."

Despite the magnitude of the information they'd just received, Molly, Devon, and Luke passed out almost immediately on the plane and slept almost the entire flight. There was only so much trauma the body could take. Only so many stresses it could compartmentalize and handle before little pieces of it began shutting down. Rae watched them snoring away, with a fond little smile; taking a strange comfort in the fact that, for once, they were all doing something normal.

The only one who was still awake was Julian. He'd been staring out the window since take-off, tracing random shapes, and generally ignoring everyone else around him.

When Rae poked him in the ribs, he looked up with a little smile. "Hey, sorry, did you say something?"

She grinned and rested her head on his shoulder. "Nope, just bored, thinking about Guilder and the awesome welcome party we're sure to get."

He chuckled. "Yeah, I wonder if they're camped out in the airport. For all we know, we could go through customs in chains."

"I'm thinking a leash," Rae mused. "Something where they can still make us work, but it's not like we can go anywhere unescorted." They laughed, and lapsed into thoughtful silence for a while before she guessed, "You thinking about Angel?"

He nodded, a warm smile spreading across his face. "Is it weird that after everything we've been through on this trip, all the terrible things that have happened, the terrible things we've learned, I'm actually going home happy?"

Rae grinned back, squeezing his arm as she also gazed out the window. "No. I think it's wonderful. No one deserves it more than you, Jules."

"I want to ask you so bad what you saw in her head," he admitted. "It's all I can think about. But I know firsthand what it's like to have the privacy of your thoughts taken away from you. I wouldn't want to do that to her."

Rae frowned thoughtfully, thinking it over. "Jules, usually when I use Carter's ink, I'm just along for the ride; I go wherever the thoughts take me. But with Angel it was all right there up in front. I think she wanted me to know. She wanted *you* to know. To believe her."

He leaned back with a sigh. "I do believe her, I just...I don't understand. I don't understand how she could actually love me, but still do that to me. Betray me and my friends to our worst enemy in the morning, and then kiss me at night. I don't get it."

Rae nodded sympathetically. "Yeah, I can imagine." Her face clouded over as flashes of the trauma she'd seen in Angel's childhood flashed through her mind. "She never had a choice, Jules. Not for a second. Her entire life was destined before it began; she was given to Cromfield as some kind of child apprentice. At first, she didn't know what she was doing. And later, she was in too deep to stop. The only thing she had a choice about was you."

Julian stared at her intently, thinking it over, before he said, "But she chose to betray me."

Rae smiled and shook her head. "She chose not to give up on her love for you. Once everything was finally out in the open, once she realized she might lose you, she told us everything we wanted to know. Even if it meant saying goodbye to everything else she'd ever known. Even if it meant that Cromfield might kill her. She chose you."

A dazzling smile spread across Julian's face, and he turned back to the window to self-consciously hide it. "I wish—I wish so badly that I could bring her back with us to England. Let the Privy Council give her protection." He turned around suddenly and looked at Rae with a hopeful expression. "Do you think if I talked to Carter, that he would—?"

"Honestly, Jules, I think none of us is in any position to be asking favors from Carter or the Privy Council."

He laughed nervously. "Yeah, that's probably true."

"But, hey," she nudged him, "maybe later. In a few weeks? A few months? Who knows what can happen? You guys have your whole lives in front..."

She didn't know where it came from. One second, she was talking to Julian, genuinely happy for him and his newfound love. The next, she was speechless, with tears in her eyes.

"Hey," he wrapped his arm around her in concern, "what's the matter? You okay?"

She pulled in a silent gasp of air and tried to smile, but the tears just kept falling. "Yeah, yeah, I'm fine. Sorry," she wiped her face, but to no avail. "I don't know what's wrong with me."

Julian's eyes softened sympathetically. "It's Devon, isn't it? You and Devon?"

Rae doubled over with a silent sob and he pulled her up against his side, holding the side of her head with a calming hand. "It's okay, it's okay," he said softly. "You're okay."

A concerned flight attendant stopped in the aisle, but he waved her away.

"Jules," Rae finally breathed, pulling herself together, "do you see a future for me?"

He sighed deeply. "I see nothing *but* a future for you."

Her throat seized up and she turned away to wipe her face. "This just can't be happening. I can't be...immortal." Her long dark hair spilled into her lap as she bowed her head. "It's so weird, sometimes it's like I just forget, you know? And everything goes back to normal. But then something will happen and I'll remember it all over again." Her breath caught in her throat, choking her. "And Devon...it's breaking my heart."

"What does Devon say about it?" he asked quietly, still squeezing her shoulders.

She sighed. "He says we'll figure it out. That we've faced worse than this before, and that if anyone can figure it out, it's the two of us."

"He's right," Julian said gently. "I know it might not be what you want to hear right now, but he's absolutely right."

She wiped her eyes again and tried to put on a brave smile. "It's stupid for me to even be talking about it, now that we know Cromfield's running around with a million different super-powers and he can't die. We don't know where the hell he is, or how to stop him."

"Hey, it's not stupid." She scoffed and Julian tilted her chin up to look at him. "It's *not* stupid," he said again. "This is your life. You know, as one of your best friends, that's pretty much top of my list of priorities."

She grinned ruefully. "Right below getting Molly to step off your love life?"

He laughed aloud. "Yeah, right below that."

There was a low groan as the plane's landing gear slowly lowered down.

"Ladies and gentlemen, we will be starting our final descent into Heathrow International Airport. Please make sure your tables and chairs are in the upright and locked position..."

"What do you think?" Rae asked, gesturing to their sleeping companions. "Should we wake them?"

"Nah—they've got a few more minutes. Let them sleep."

It wasn't until the plane touched down on the runway, sending up sprays of water on both sides, that Julian finally turned back to her.

"And Rae, about Cromfield..." His eyes shone with an abnormal intensity as they locked onto hers. "He can die. Everything can die. We just need to figure out how."

Rae nodded automatically, and dropped her head on his shoulder as she stared outside at the trees blurring past the edge of the runway.

She certainly hoped he was right.

The five friends thought they would see members of the Privy Council lined up outside the gate when they stepped off the plane—they were wrong. They thought they'd see Carter, and Bethany Kerrigan, standing with guns blazing outside the baggage check, but wrong again.

They found Devon's car in long-term parking and headed home in silence, pausing only to drop Luke off along the way.

"Well, good luck, you guys," he said a little nervously. "If I don't hear from you for a couple of weeks, I'll assume they just dumped the bodies."

They laughed and drove away, but, under the joke, all of them were nervous. The Privy Council was not a group to let this sort of disobedience just passively slide. And they were not the kind to wait for the wrongdoer to come to them either. They were proactive. Collectors. Punishers. And neither Devon, Rae, Julian, nor Molly could come up with a reason that they hadn't been picked up yet.

When they finally pulled onto Guilder grounds, it was the same thing. The school was a dead zone. Of course, they'd half expected this. School was out for the summer, and, by now, all the remaining students would have long since left. But the Privy Council still trained and operated here, and there was not a soul to be seen. Not even a lone groundskeeper as they pulled up the ghostly drive.

"Alright," Molly muttered, "this is starting to really creep me out. Where's Madame Elpis? She lives here full time and I don't even see *her* car here."

Devon frowned worriedly. "I don't know." He pulled the car around and headed out of Guilder. "Let's head to the Privy Council building.

He drove, and they all sat in silence, even as Devon pulled into a parking space not far from the Tudor-style home that had been converted into the Privy Council office. "Let's try here first. Then the training facility."

The four of them got out in silence, and began the long walk across parking lot. The front doors were locked.

Jules looked around. "Training facility?"

Devon and Rae nodded at the same time.

Molly sighed. "Can we just walk there? I'm tired of sitting."

"Sure, Molls." Rae slipped around her friends and led the way to the half hidden entrance and punched in the security code to the entrance and then again in the training facility.

It was dark when they stepped inside. Devon flipped the lights in the main gym, but nothing happened. He glanced back at them with a shrug, and the four of them proceeded across the gymnasium floor to the halls in shadowed darkness on the other side of the gym. It wasn't until they reached the main conference room that they finally saw a light and heard some voices from behind the closed door.

"Thank goodness," Molly muttered. "I was starting to think zombie apocalypse."

Devon glanced back at the others before his eyes fell on Rae. "You ready to do this?"

She sighed. "Do we have a choice?"

He flashed her a little smile before pushing open the door.

It was like flipping a switch. Every single person in the room froze the second they stepped inside. And it was *every single person*. All the missing people Rae had yet to see on Guilder grounds.

Madame Elpis was standing in a corner with several members of the faculty. Dean Wardell was hunched over in an easy chair—avoiding eye contact with everyone. Carter was sitting behind his desk, surrounded by minions, and Beth was sitting by his side. It was clear she'd been crying.

"Mom?" Rae asked fearfully. "What's—"

Carter stood up with a grave look on his face as two armed guards appeared from just behind the door and grabbed Rae by the arms. She stifled a gasp of surprise and froze in place just like everyone else, staring at the room with wide, bewildered eyes.

"Rae Kerrigan?" one of the guards thundered.

Rae didn't think she'd ever been more terrified to hear her own name. "Y-Yes?"

For a split second, she met Devon's eyes.

Then the whole world came tumbling down.

"You're under arrest, Ms. Kerrigan."

Wait? What? She struggled against them, and considered using a tatù, but hesitated as she hissed, "What the hell's going on?"

THE END
Twisted Together
Coming out in February 2016

Note from Author

I can't believe HIDDEN DARKNESS is finished! It barely seemed like yesterday and I was thinking about Rae and what she would do if she had this tattoo that give her supernatural powers. Now I'm working on book 9 of this series!! (10 if you include the prequel lol)

I hope you enjoyed Rae's story as it continues. If you have a moment to post a review to let others know about the story, I'd greatly appreciate it!

I love hearing from my fans so feel free to send me a message on Facebook or by email so we can chat!

I'm working on Twisted Together and have am imagining what Beth and Simon went through before Rae was born. Crazy crazy crazy world!! And I love it!!

All the best, W.J. May

Newsletter: http://eepurl.com/97aYf

Website: http://www.wanitamay.yolasite.com

Facebook: https://www.facebook.com/pages/Author-WJ-May-FAN-PAGE/141170442608149

The Chronicles of Kerrigan

Book I - *Rae of Hope* is FREE!
   Book Trailer:
   http://www.youtube.com/watch?v=gILAwXxx8MU
   Book II - *Dark Nebula*
   Book Trailer:
   http://www.youtube.com/watch?v=Ca24STi_bFM
   Book III - *House of Cards*
   Book IV - *Royal Tea*
   Book V - *Under Fire*
   Book VI - *End in Sight*
   Book VII – *Hidden Darkness*
   Book VIII – *Twisted Together*
   COMING FEBRUARY 2016
   PREQUEL – Christmas Before the Magic

Coming Christmas 2015!!

A Novella of the Chronicles of Kerrigan.
A prequel on how Simon Kerrigan met Beth!!
AVAILABLE for 99 Cents
LIMITED TIME!

More books by W.J. May

Hidden Secrets Saga:
Download Seventh Mark part 1 For FREE
Book Trailer:
http://www.youtube.com/watch?v=Y- vVYC1gvo

Like most teenagers, Rouge is trying to figure out who she is and what she wants to be. With little knowledge about her past, she has questions but has never tried to find the answers. Everything changes when she befriends a strangely intoxicating family. Siblings Grace and Michael, appear to have secrets which seem connected to Rouge. Her hunch is confirmed when a horrible incident occurs at an outdoor party. Rouge may be the only one who can find the answer.

An ancient journal, a Sioghra necklace and a special mark force life-altering decisions for a girl who grew up unprepared to fight for her life or others.

All secrets have a cost and Rouge's determination to find the truth can only lead to trouble...or something even more sinister.

RADIUM HALOS - THE SENSELESS SERIES
Book 1 is FREE:

Book Blurb:

Everyone needs to be a hero at one point in their life.

The small town of Elliot Lake will never be the same again.

Caught in a sudden thunderstorm, Zoe, a high school senior from Elliot Lake, and five of her friends take shelter in an abandoned uranium mine. Over the next few days, Zoe's hearing sharpens drastically, beyond what any normal human being can detect. She tells her friends, only to learn that four others have an increased sense as well. Only Kieran, the new boy from Scotland, isn't affected.

Fashioning themselves into superheroes, the group tries to stop the strange occurrences happening in their little town. Muggings, break-ins, disappearances, and murder begin to hit too close to home. It leads the team to think someone knows about their secret - someone who wants them all dead.

An incredulous group of heroes. A traitor in the midst. Some dreams are written in blood.

Shadow of Doubt
Part 1 is FREE!
Book Trailer:
http://www.youtube.com/watch?v=LZK09Fe7kgA

Book Blurb:

What happens when you fall for the one you are forbidden to love?

Erebus is a bit of a lost soul. He's a guy so he should be out to have fun but unlike the rest of his kind, he is solemn and withdrawn. That is, until he meets Aurora, a law student at Cornell University. His entire world is shaken. Feelings he's never had and urges he's never understood take over. These strange longings drive him to question everything about himself

When a jealous ex stalks back into his life, he must decide if he is willing to risk everything to be with Aurora. His desire for her could destroy her, or worse, erase his own existence forever.

Courage Runs Red
The Blood Red Series
Book 1 is FREE

What if courage was your only option?

When Kallie lands a college interview with the city's new hot-shot police officer, she has no idea everything in her life is about to change. The detective is young, handsome and seems to have an unnatural ability to stop the increasing local crime rate. Detective Liam's particular interest in Kallie sends her heart and head stumbling over each other.

When a raging blood feud between vampires spills into her home, Kallie gets caught in the middle. Torn between love and family loyalty she must find the courage to fight what she fears the most and possibly risk everything, even if it means dying for those she loves.

Free Books:

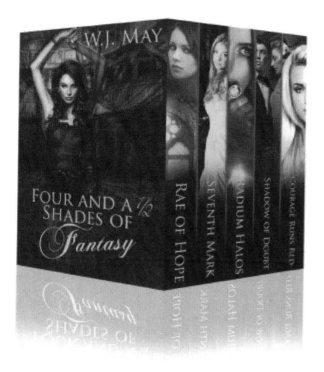

Four and a Half Shades of Fantasy

TUDOR COMPARISON:

Aumbry House——A recess to hold sacred vessels, often found in castle chapels.

Aumbry House was considered very special to hold the female students - their sacred vessels (especially Rae Kerrigan).

Joist House——A timber stretched from wall-to-wall to support floorboards.

Joist House was considered a building of support where the male students could support and help each other.

Oratory——A private chapel in a house.

Private education room in the school where the students were able to practice their gifting and improve their skills. Also used as a banquet - dance hall when needed.

Oriel——A projecting window in a wall; originally a form of porch, often of wood. The original bay windows of the Tudor period. Guilder College majority of windows were oriel.

Rae often felt her life was being watching through one of these windows. Hence the constant reference to them.

Refectory——A communal dining hall. Same termed used in Tudor times.

Scriptorium——A Medieval writing room in which scrolls were also housed.

Used for English classes and still store some of the older books from the Tudor reign (regarding tatùs).

Privy Council——Secret council and "arm of the government" similar to the CIA, etc... In Tudor times, the Privy Council was King Henry's board of advisors and helped run the country.

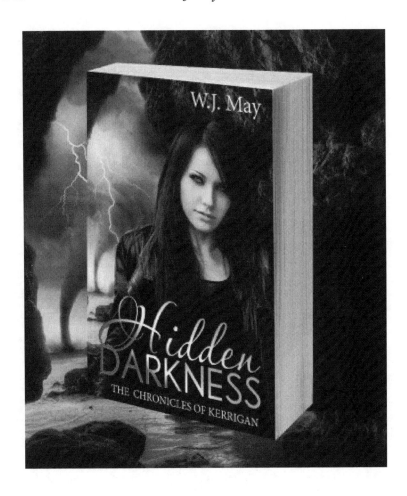

Don't miss out!

Click the button below and you can sign up to receive emails whenever W.J. May publishes a new book. There's no charge and no obligation.

Did you love *Hidden Darkness*? Then you should read *Christmas Before the Magic* by W.J. May!

Learn how it all began ... before the magic of tatùs.

When Argyle invites his best friend, Simon Kerrigan, home for the Christmas holidays, he wants to save Simon from staying at Guilder Boarding School on his own.

Simon comes along and doesn't expect to find much more excitement in the tiny Scottish town where Argyle's family lives. Until he meets Beth, Argyle's older sister. She's beautiful, brash and clearly interested in him.

When her father warns him to stay away from her, Simon tries, but sometimes destiny has a hope of it's own.

The Chronicles of Kerrigan Prequel is the beginning of the story before Rae Kerrigan. This Christmas Novella is the start (but it may not be the end...)

The	Chronicles	of	Kerrigan	Series
Rae		of		Hope
Dark				Nebula
House		of		Cards
Royal				Tea
Under				Fire
End		in		Sight
Hidden				Darkness
Twisted Together				

Also by W.J. May

Bit-Lit Series
Lost Vampire
Cost of Blood
Price of Death

Blood Red Series
Courage Runs Red
The Night Watch

Daughters of Darkness: Victoria's Journey
Huntress
Coveted (A Vampire & Paranormal Romance)
Victoria

Hidden Secrets Saga
Seventh Mark - Part 1
Seventh Mark - Part 2
Marked By Destiny
Compelled
Fate's Intervention
Chosen Three

The Chronicles of Kerrigan
Rae of Hope
Dark Nebula
House of Cards
Royal Tea
Under Fire
End in Sight

Hidden Darkness

The Chronicles of Kerrigan Prequel
Christmas Before the Magic

The Hidden Secrets Saga
Seventh Mark (part 1 & 2)

The Senseless Series
Radium Halos
Radium Halos - Part 2
Nonsense

The X Files
Replica X

Standalone
Shadow of Doubt (Part 1 & 2)
Five Shades of Fantasy
Glow - A Young Adult Fantasy Sampler
Shadow of Doubt - Part 2
Four and a Half Shades of Fantasy
Full Moon
Dream Fighter
What Creeps in the Night
Forest of the Forbidden
HuNted
Arcane Forest: A Fantasy Anthology
Ancient Blood of the Vampire and Werewolf

Made in the USA
San Bernardino, CA
26 January 2016

J. M. Coetzee, 1984. Copyright 1989 by Dick Penner Studios, Knoxville, Tennessee.

COUNTRIES
OF THE MIND